Home Child

Home Child

Barbara Haworth-Attard

Cover design by Dan Clark

ROUSSAN
PUBLISHERS INC.
Specializing in YA and fiction for pre-teens

Roussan Publishers Inc. acknowledges with appreciation the assistance of the Book Publishing Industry Development Program of Canadian Heritage and the Canada Council in the production of this book.

http://www.magnet.ca/roussan

Copyright © 1996 by Barbara Haworth-Attard

Legal deposit 4th quarter 1996
National Library of Canada
Quebec National Library

Canadian Cataloguing in Publication Data
Haworth-Attard, Barbara 1953-
Home child
(On time's wing)
ISBN 1-896184-18-9
1. Child immigrants–Ontario–History–Juvenile fiction.
2. British–Ontario–History–Juvenile fiction.
I. Title. II. Series
PS8565.A865H64 1996 jC813'.54 C96-900916-X
PZ7.H313565Ho 1996

Cover design by Dan Clark.
Cover photo courtesy of
McCord Museum of Canadian History, Notman Photographic Archives.
Interior design by Jean Shepherd

Poem page 61, *Selections from Irving and Hawthorne*. "The Voyage",
Washington Irving, The Copp Clark Literature Series. ©1915.
The Copp Clark Company Limited, Toronto, Ontario.

Poem page 78, "Snow", Author Unknown, *The Ontario Readers First Book*
©1909. The T. Eaton Co. Ltd.

Published simultaneously in Canada and the United States of America.

Printed in Canada

2 3 4 5 6 7 8 9 MRQ 9 8 7 6

DEDICATION

For John Atterbury, Surviving Home Child
A remarkable man, a remarkable spirit

Author's Acknowledgements

Many people helped me with the research required to write this book, but I wish to extend a special thank you to David Lorente, Heritage Renfrew Home Children (Canada) Committee, Austin Hodgins for his historical/ farm expertise, Dr. John Waters for the loan of his family diaries, Liz Hardin of Doon Heritage Crossroads and most importantly, thank you to all the Home Children and their descendants who opened their homes and hearts to me.

Permissions to quote from historical articles and letters appearing at the chapter headings have been generously provided by the following organizations:

Anne of Green Gables is a trademark and official mark of the Anne of Green Gables Licensing Authority Inc., which is owned by the heirs of L.M. Montgomery and the Province of Prince Edward Island and located in Charlottetown, Prince Edward Island.

The Catholic Children's Society (Diocese of Westminster), London, England. (Formerly The Crusade of Rescue).

The Globe and Mail, reprinted with permission.

The London Free Press, reproduced with permission. Further reproduction without written permission from the *London Free Press* is prohibited.

Dear Reader,

For some reason, you have never been taught about the one hundred thousand children—most between seven and fourteen, some older, many mere toddlers—who were literally exported by Britain to Canada as cheap farm labor until the Great Depression. You may not even know that many are alive today and until recently they were ashamed to admit they were Home Children.

Home Children seldom talk of their past and this book suggests why. At the turn of the century many Canadians believed in applying eugenics to humans to keep our "bloodlines pure". As a result they inflicted a cruel and unjust stigma on Home Children who, because they were poor, were ripped from family and familiar surroundings in Britain and sent to slave on farms in Canada. How was a mere child to respond to such treatment? Who could understand how the child really felt?

Barbara Haworth-Attard has somehow managed to get inside the minds and hearts of Arthur, the Home Boy, and Sadie, his empathetic peer in the family to which he was sent.

From my own experience in talking to and corresponding with thousands of Home Children and their descendants, I can say that Ms Haworth-Attard has touched all the right buttons.

This sensitive story is not just for children. Home Children, their descendants and friends will welcome it and those who know nothing of the Home Children story will be amazed that such things could have happened in Canada.

J.A. David Lorente, Chair
Heritage Renfrew Home Children
Canada Committee

At first Matthew suggested getting a Home boy. But I said "no" flat to that. "They may be all right—I'm not saying they're not—but no London street Arabs for me," I said. "Give me a native born at least. There'll be a risk, no matter who we get. But I'll feel easier in my mind and sleep sounder at nights if we get a born Canadian."

Marilla Cuthbert
Anne of Green Gables © 1908

CHAPTER 1

"Calf's dead." Mr. Wilson stomped into the kitchen and kicked off his barn boots by the porch door.

Sadie took one look at her father's face, thundercloud black with anger, and hurriedly set a large bowl of porridge on the table. She placed a small pitcher of maple syrup next to it. Dad's *indulgence*, Mama called it.

"Can't see any clear reason for it. Cow seemed healthy throughout." He picked up the pitcher and poured a steady stream of thick, brown liquid over the porridge. Lucky thing, Sadie thought watching him, that it had been a good year for maple syrup. Sunny days and frosty nights had kept the sap flowing from the maple trees in the back bush longer than usual this past spring.

Sadie's mother turned from the stove carrying a

plate heaped with fried potatoes, eggs and thick slices of ham. "Mary Lou's all right?" she asked anxiously, the corners of her mouth puckered with worry. "She's my best milk cow."

"Cow's fine," Sadie's father scraped up the last of his porridge, pushed the bowl aside and without stopping to take a breath, shoved a forkful of potatoes into his mouth.

He'd been up all night with the calving, Sadie knew, then had milked the cows himself, a job she and her older sister, Laura, usually did. He must want nothing more than to tumble into bed, but the day had started and there was too much to do.

Grandma Wilson shuffled into the kitchen, slippers swishing across the floor. She couldn't lift up her feet any more because of her swollen knee joints. Shrewd, brown eyes narrowed as she peered at Mr. Wilson. Lost the calf," she said, shaking her head. "A shame, but there'll be another along soon."

Mr. Wilson merely grunted, while Sadie's mother clucked her tongue irritably. A dead calf didn't put money in their pockets.

Sunlight fell in wide, butter yellow beams across the wooden kitchen floor. An early morning breeze felt cool through the screened porch door, but later, Sadie knew, the August sun would be white hot and straight overhead, heating the air until she could barely breathe. She listened to the rhythmic *thump-thump* of Laura kneading dough for bread, admiring the deft way in which her sister flipped the soft, white mass into one hand, while the other scattered flour over the board in a single, smooth motion. And hated her for it.

Her own attempts to make bread looked clumsy next to Laura's, leaving Mama angry and impatient. No matter how much she tried, Sadie could not get the dough to stretch and glisten like her sister's. To make matters worse, Laura would roll her eyes and sigh hugely at the grey, soggy mess that Sadie punched and pounded with no success. A waste of good food, Mama scolded, but still she always made Sadie try again. Every woman had to know how to make bread, preparing for the day she ran her own household.

"Haven't you got those eggs yet?" Mrs. Wilson's voice cut shrill through the quiet kitchen.

Sadie whirled about to see her younger sister, Amy, standing outside the screened door, nervously shifting a basket from hand to hand. An empty basket.

"I'll help her, Mama," Sadie said quickly. She hustled Amy off the porch and pushed the small girl in front of her across the yard.

"The big hen won't leave the chicken coop," Amy said tearfully.

"Did you spread their feed outside like I told you?" Sadie asked.

"Yes, but she still won't leave."

Sadie waded through chickens pecking at corn and crumbs in the yard, bent double and passed through the small door leading into the coop. The air inside was sharp and burned her eyes. A fat, old hen spread her wings and cackled at her fiercely, but Sadie shouted and flapped her own arms, chasing the hen outside.

"It's safe now," she called and waited, but Amy didn't come in. Sadie poked her head out the door. "Come on!"

Amy looked at the rooster strutting about the yard.

"He won't hurt you," Sadie said impatiently. She ducked back into the coop and searched the nests for eggs, folding her apron into a pouch to carry them. Apron full, she turned to leave, when a sudden tugging sensation followed by a loud ripping sound stopped her. She looked with dismay from a rusted nail to a long tear in her dress. Maybe if she kept her apron on, Mama might not notice. It was very important that she not make Mama mad today. Today, she and Dad were going to town to pick up their Home child.

The McMillans on the next concession road had taken in an orphan boy from England a year ago to help on the farm. The boy never came to school, but Sadie saw him at church most Sundays. Unkempt and rail-thin, he kept to himself, not mixing with the other churchgoers who gathered after services to exchange news. Lately Sadie had seen her father speaking a great deal to Mr. McMillan and, listening at the stovepipe hole in the floor of Grandma's room one evening, she'd discovered the reason for those talks. Plain as plain she heard Mr. Wilson's announcement that he'd sent a request for a Home child and one would be arriving shortly. Mama had been furious.

Sadie had taken to listening at the stovepipe hole since she had first become aware that a secret lived in her house. Not a secret like the kind a person hugged joyfully to themselves or happily surprised others with, but a dark secret that lurked uneasily in the corners of the kitchen and hid unspoken beneath the daily chores. But no matter how hard she looked or listened, she couldn't find the secret. Only knew it was there.

She heard a lot from that pipe in the floor above the kitchen, though not all of it to her liking. Just the night before she had heard her mother and father arguing.

"I still don't see why you want a Home child," Mama said angrily.

"Been over this already," Dad replied. "Need a boy to help with the farmwork."

"Well, he'll just be trouble. Those boys are picked up right off the city streets of England, or taken from the workhouses and sent over here. Orphans, with no decent upbringing, or with no-good parents who can't even care for their own. Thieves, the whole lot of them. Shipping out their riffraff is what England is doing. Sending us their problem so they don't have to deal with it themselves," Mama sniffed.

"Asked for a boy of thirteen," Dad said. "Big enough to help with the chores but, if need be, not too big to have the thieving knocked out of him."

Baby Lizzie started crying then, drowning out Mama's voice, but Sadie heard her father's next words plain as plain. "Another girl," he said before Lizzie's screams echoed up the pipe and Sadie could no longer hear. No, not everything she heard through the stove-pipe hole was to her liking.

~~~

Sadie's father finished his dinner, then pushed back his chair. "I'll be off now," he said. "Anything you need picked up in town?"

"Laura, get the butter crock from the basement," Mrs. Wilson ordered. "I have butter and eggs to sell in town and I need flour and sugar. I've written every-thing here." She handed him a list as he went out the door. Head down, shoulders hunched to make herself look smaller, Sadie sidled after him, holding her apron tightly over the skirt of her dress.

"Where are you off to, girl?" Mama asked.

Sadie stopped. "Dad said I could go to town with him."

Her mother stared at her, lips clamped in a tight, straight line. Laura stood behind looking at her with disapproval. Wishing she could go, Sadie thought.

"I heard him tell her so myself, Aggie," Grandma Wilson said.

Sadie's mother shook her head. "There's a lot you could be helping with around here instead of running to town. The garden needs hoeing..." Suddenly, she threw her hands up in the air. "Very well, then. Go!"

Sadie let out a pent-up breath and headed for the door.

"Are you wearing your apron to town?" Laura asked sweetly, a tiny smile curving her lips.

She'd seen the tear, Sadie realized. Mama would never let her go now.

Grandma Wilson struggled out of her rocking chair. "I need some wool matched in town, Sadie. Come up to my room and I'll find the color."

Sadie hurriedly followed Grandma up the stairs. In the bedroom, the old woman twitched Sadie's apron aside and eyed the long rip. "Good gracious, girl," she said, shaking her head. "Thread a needle for me. My eyes are too old to see the hole."

Sadie's fingers shook as she poked the thread through the needle's eye. She could hear her father leading the horses from the barn, talking to them softly about the coming trip to town. He'd go without her if she wasn't down soon. She craned her neck to see out the window.

"Stand still," Grandma Wilson ordered. Crooked fingers rapidly stitched the tear.

Running through the kitchen with a length of blue wool dangling from her fingers, Sadie felt the urge to laugh at the surprise in Laura's face at seeing the apron and tear gone, but she kept her own face straight until the porch door banged behind her. Smiling widely, she climbed up beside her father onto the wagon seat.

Sixty-five English boys, ranging in ages from 11 to 18 have arrived in Canada in care of the Barnardo home. The boys were undaunted at finding themselves in new and strange surroundings and took to their new home like ducks to water.

Stratford Beacon Herald
April 27, 1928
Stratford, Ontario

Mr. Wilson's head nodded lower, chin bouncing gently on his chest as he dozed, reins held loosely in his hands. Sadie wasn't worried. Jake and Sam, their work horses, could find the way to and from town in a blinding blizzard all by themselves if necessary. She watched their solid, wide backs sway as they plodded up the dirt road, heavy feet stirring up clouds of brown dust that caught in her throat. Sweat trickled down Sadie's back, leaving her itchy and uncomfortable, but she didn't mind. She'd rather be itchy and uncomfortable on the way to town than back home under Mama's watchful eye.

They passed the Thompson farm where Sadie saw the five Thompson boys working. The binder moved steadily through a field, oats falling in wide swaths. Mr. Thompson and the oldest boy, James, followed behind standing the bundles of grain into stooks to dry. Nearer the road the younger boys strung new wire between the posts of a broken fence. They stopped working to watch the wagon pass, but Sadie didn't bother waving. She didn't like the brothers much. They swaggered about the schoolyard bossing and bullying the other children, feeling safe in their numbers. But still—she shaded her eyes with one hand and squinted through the sun's glare—the two biggest were able to do a man's work, something Mr. Thompson would be grateful for.

If they hadn't been going to town, Dad would be cutting their own oats, with Amy, Laura and herself, and any hired help Dad could find, standing the grain into stooks. She looked over at her father. *Another girl.* He wanted a boy to help work the farm.

She'd always known this deep down, but still, it had hurt to hear those words through the stovepipe hole. She tried her best to help him, but it must not be good enough, because here they were on their way to town to get a Home boy. She wasn't much use to him, being a girl.

The wagon drew past large homes set back from the road by wide green lawns, then smaller wooden and brick houses crowded together. An automobile swept past in a swirl of dust and noise. Jake shook his head irritably, but didn't break his steady stride. Mr. Wilson snorted, blinked and gathered the reins in his hand. "Here already are we?" he said.

A three-storey grey building with four tall columns flanking a double door and carvings etched high in the walls near the roof caught Sadie's eye. Passing that building meant they were near downtown. The horses' hooves sounded a loud *clop-clop* as dirt gave way to pavement in the city's centre. Sadie craned her neck every way looking at buildings, into store windows, and up at telephone and electric wires stretching from tall poles at the side of the road to crisscross overhead in a black, cat's cradle string game. She still couldn't figure out how those wires made a light shine steady without coal oil or a voice get inside a skinny wooden box on the kitchen wall.

She saw a large sign with *Sunlight Soap* printed on it. Some people bought soap; Mama made theirs from ashes. People hurried in and out of buildings, crossed streets and strode rapidly down sidewalks, weaving their way in and around each other with intricate steps like dancers. Town noise pressed hard on ears used to country quiet.

"Break your neck gawking about like that," Mr. Wilson said.

Sadie laughed. She'd been downtown many times before but could never get her fill of it.

Mr. Wilson eased the horses to the right of the shiny, metal electric streetcar tracks. A police officer waved them through a busy intersection, one hand stopping the oncoming vehicles so they could pass safely. Around a corner and the Grand Trunk Railway building loomed before them.

Sadie followed her father, dodging people who pulled and pummelled bags and parcels through the station's wide doors. One majestic woman sailed through the crowds in the station with an enormous, flower and feather hat perched on her head. Watching her, Sadie stumbled and bumped into a man. A face frowned at her from above a high, white collar and knotted tie that squeezed neck and cheeks to a beet red. Sadie murmured an apology and hurried away.

"Stout country girl," came floating after her and Sadie flushed. At one time being born with plain brown hair and matching brown eyes meant easily fading into the background, but lately she'd had what Mama called a *growth spurt*. It seemed every morning when she awoke her legs stretched longer and her body broader. Now everyone noticed her. With relief she came out onto the wide train platform to find her father studying his pocket watch. If maple syrup was Dad's indulgence, the pocket watch was his pride and joy.

Passed on to him from his father, the watch hung from a loop in a gold chain that fastened to a pocket for safekeeping. By pressing in a precise spot, the engraved gold top would spring open, revealing two sturdy hands solemnly marching through time. Around and around. He snapped the watch shut and pushed it back into his pocket so only the chain remained showing and looked around the station. "Train's been already," he said.

Two ragged lines of uniformed men stood talking and laughing with each other, but immediately fell silent, stiffened their backs and spaced themselves with precision at the approach of a single man, also uniformed with medals pinned to his chest.

Sadie shook her father's arm. "Look Dad, soldiers." Her eyes widened at the sight of their rifles. "Are they going to the war?"

"Looks like it," Mr. Wilson replied absently. England declaring war on Germany two weeks before had been of little interest to him, his only concern being the coming shortage of hired hands as young men signed up to be soldiers.

Sadie looked around and felt a moment's disappointment upon seeing that the train had already left, but it quickly disappeared when she caught a glimpse of a cluster of children waiting at the far end of the platform.

There were eight of them, all looking the same; the boys in grey, wool pants and navy jackets with matching cloth caps, and the girls in blue dresses, navy coats and felt hats squashed on their heads. But it wasn't only their clothes that made them look similar, it was also their faces; paste white, with deep, purple circles drawn under dulled eyes. Sadie looked at her own plump arm, seeing the summer-gold skin.

There was no laughing or chatter, only the occasional backward look as one by one they were led off until only a boy remained. Mr. Wilson stared at him a moment, then gestured to the boy to follow.

∽∽∽

"Your name again, boy?" Sadie's father hu-upped to the horses to move them smartly down the dirt road. Getting Grandma's wool matched and Mrs. Wilson's list filled had taken longer than expected.

"Arthur, sir." The voice from the back of the wagon was flat and low, barely a whisper.

Sadie turned to stare at the boy huddled between feed bags and a small, brown trunk. It was the first he had spoken since they had picked him up from the train station, and that was easily three miles back.

"And you're thirteen?" Mr. Wilson said.

"Yes, sir."

"Hmph! Pretty small for thirteen. Look to be ten—eleven at most."

Sadie glanced at her father from the corner of her eye. Why was he asking all these questions? He knew the boy's name and age; the Children's Agency had told them all that. Maybe he was just checking to make sure they had picked up the proper one.

Her father was right though—Sadie studied the boy critically—he was awful skinny and weak looking. A year older than her, yet she bet she could flatten him onto his back easily—and keep him there. But then, she was big for her age.

The boy gripped a brown satchel tight to his chest. Sadie eyed it curiously. The way he held it so close, there must be important things inside—she felt a stirring of excitement—things from England.

The navy cap slipped sideways exposing a blonde stubble on the boy's head. Maybe that was what made him seem so young, having no hair. Sadie knew why he looked like this.

"I don't want bugs in my house," her mother had said. Sadie, her ear pressed to the stovepipe opening, had heard the Home Visitor from the Children's Agency assure her mother there would be none. That had been the day when Dad had signed the paper giving them a Home boy. Sadie looked doubtfully at Arthur. Maybe her father had forgotten to tell the Visiting Lady that everyone worked hard on their farm.

The wagon lurched in a deep rut and the boy rolled, banging his knee hard into the wooden side boards. It must have hurt, but he didn't take any notice. Just like he didn't notice the tall, blue chicory bending from the sides of the road or the snow white fields of Queen Anne's lace. Merely held tight to his bag and stared at his hands.

Sadie began to feel disappointed. She'd been looking forward all week to having a Home child stay with them. Especially one who might be a thief. Now he was here and he didn't seem all that interesting.

"They call you Art, or Artie?" Sadie's father asked.

"Arthur," the boy replied.

"Use your full name, eh?"

"It's a king's name," Arthur muttered.

Sadie's head whirled about to stare at the boy again. She had never known anybody named for a king before! Sky blue eyes looked directly at her this time, a white spark gleaming in the middle of them. Anger? Sadie wondered.

"A king's name." Mr. Wilson laughed shortly. "Well, only pigs and cows and chickens on our farm. Fine surroundings for royalty."

Arthur's face flushed a deep red as he lowered his head and fixed his eyes on his hands once again.

I would ask that you not expect too much from these children....they may be full of defects that require eradicating, and perhaps of virtues that should be developed.

Letter from Guthrie Home,
London, Ontario to farmer
taking in a Home Child, 1887

Dusk softened the stark, hard edges of the yard as the wagon pulled up the lane. The sun hung low in the west sky, a large, red ball washing the yellow-brick farmhouse in pink. Old Bob wobbled out from the barn on four stiff legs to watch their arrival. The new puppy, Patches, jumped excitedly around the older dog, barking and nipping at the horses' legs until a shouted word from Mr. Wilson sent him slinking away. Sadie climbed down from the wagon and ran up the back porch steps leading to the kitchen. Arthur followed, struggling with his trunk and satchel. The room was moist and hot from cooking, and good smells made Sadie's stomach rumble hungrily. Stealing a glance at the wrung-out boy beside her, she guessed he felt pretty much the same.

Laura was cutting thick slices from a brown capped loaf of bread, while Amy carefully lined up forks and

24

knives on the table. Baby Lizzie fretted in the cradle.

"You're late," Sadie's mother said. A bead of perspiration trembled on the end of her nose. "Lend me a hand here to get this supper out. Why you had to go to town when you know I needed you here..."

"This is Arthur, Mama," Sadie interrupted. She hurriedly picked up a bowl of carrots and put them on the table.

"So I supposed," her mother replied. She didn't turn from the stove.

"He's come from Great Britain, Mama." Sadie tried again.

"I know." A platter of meat was shoved into Sadie's hand. "Put that by your father's plate."

Arthur stood in the middle of the hot kitchen clutching his bag in one hand and his cap in the other, looking for all the world like he would fall apart if he took another step.

Sadie's mother heaped a plate with food and held it out to him. "Here boy," she said. "I won't have anybody saying I starved a Home child."

Arthur stuffed his cap into his jacket pocket and took the plate. "Thank you," he said as he bobbed his head and started toward the table.

Mrs. Wilson's voice stopped him. "You take that plate and eat over there." She pointed to a stool set near the stove in the corner of the kitchen.

Arthur stared at Sadie's mother a long moment, then slowly the color drained from his blue eyes. His face emptied of expression to become as blank as a new page waiting for printing. To Sadie it seemed like he'd locked himself far away from them.

"Yes Ma'am," he mumbled. He backed toward the stove and stumbled over his trunk. Carrots rolled from his plate. He hurriedly picked them up from the floor, flopped down on the stool and awkwardly balanced his plate on one knee. Laura snickered and Sadie glared at her. Amy watched with wide eyes.

Mr. Wilson came in, crossed to the pump and washed the horse smell from his hands, then sat at the end of the table. All eyes closed for the blessing.

Sadie peeked at Arthur from under her lashes. Why did Mama tell him to eat in the corner instead of at the table? There was lots of room, especially if she kept her elbows pressed politely to her sides like Mama constantly reminded her. Was it because Arthur might be a thief that Mama didn't want him at the table? Would he steal their forks and knives? A sharp kick on the shin from Grandma's slippered foot closed Sadie's eyes.

"Lots of soldiers at the station," Sadie's father said. He spooned potatoes onto his plate. "Heading to England, then off to Europe for the war. Men rushing to sign up. Scared they'll miss it. Paper says they expect the Kaiser to be beaten by Christmas. Pack of fools if they believe that."

Sadie's mother looked up anxiously.

"It's over there, Aggie," Mr. Wilson reassured her. "Other side of the world. Besides they don't take old farmers—or," he stabbed his fork around the table at the three girls, "women for soldiers, so we've no worry." Amy jumped when the fork pointed her way. Too sensitive that girl, Grandma always said.

Sadie suddenly heard in her mind the words that had echoed up the stovepipe. *Another girl.* She quickly glanced over at her mother and saw her staring at the cradle, and knew Mama too remembered Dad's words.

Sadie's father waved his knife in the direction of the stove. "Good thing we got the boy. Won't be any hired hands around soon. All rushing off to be soldiers," he said. "Says he wants to be called Arthur. Says he's named after a king."

Arthur's fork stopped mid-way to his mouth, then slowly continued upward.

"And so he is," Grandma said. "King Arthur and the Knights of the Round Table."

Sadie stared at her grandmother with an open mouth.

"Guess you're wondering how I know that, aren't you, girl?" Grandma's breath whistled over toothless gums. "Well, my Dad came from Cornwall—Great Britain—like Arthur here. Came to Canada when I was just a wee thing. Do you remember your granddad, Thomas?" she asked Sadie's father.

"Not much. Died while I was still small."

"Anyway," Grandma continued. "As any good Cornish man will tell you, King Arthur was born in Cornwall. Dad knew all kinds of stories about him and his knights. If you asked him enough times—made a fuss over him—he'd tell you one."

Sadie looked at Arthur. He had stopped eating to stare at Grandma.

"Papers are signed for the boy to stay here a year," Mr. Wilson said.

"And if he doesn't work out?" Sadie's mother asked, standing and crossing to the counter where a golden crusted pie sat.

"The Home says to send him back. They'll pay the fare."

Mrs. Wilson turned and looked at Arthur. "I'll expect you to be polite, respectful and hardworking," she said. "And if you aren't—back you go, you understand? We'll send you back to where you came from without a second thought if you bring any shame to this house," she ended fiercely.

Stunned, Sadie listened to her mother's rising voice. How could having a Home boy bring any shame to them?

"After supper, boy," Sadie's father said. "I'll show you how to get the stock settled for the night. Be one of your chores."

"Good gracious, Thomas!" Grandma protested. "That boy has sailed across the Atlantic from England, and spent two days in a train crossing half of Canada. He's exhausted. Let him have one night to rest before you get him working."

Sadie's father angrily puffed up his cheeks, then blew out a long breath. "One night, then, but be up early in the morning. Lot of work to be done."

Again Sadie saw a look pass between Arthur and her

grandmother and this time Sadie noticed the tiny white spark flare again in the centre of Arthur's blue eyes, partly erasing the emptiness from the boy's face.

"Yeow!" Sadie yelped and rubbed knuckles left stinging from her mother's sharp rap with the back of a spoon.

"Stop staring at that Home boy," Mrs. Wilson scolded. "I don't want you having anything to do with him. He's not our sort."

"A better sort, I'd say," Sadie's grandmother cackled.

Another party of boys left over-crowded England on July 27th....What a glorious exchange they have made; the health-giving, open-air life of Canada...for the putrid air of a close court in some slum in an over-crowded town in this country.

St. Peter's Net, England, 1905

Sadie scrubbed at yellow egg yolk that had hardened solid on a plate. She felt trapped by chores—cooking and sweeping, milking and hoeing, endless fruits and vegetables to pick and put down for winter. Finish one chore and another would be waiting. She sighed deeply and dipped more hot water from the warming tank on the stove and poured it over the soap shavings in the basin.

"What are you moaning about?" Mama asked.

"I'm tired of always doing dishes," Sadie replied.

"No sense in complaining. You'll be doing them all your life. Especially when you get married and run your own household."

"Maybe I won't get married," Sadie said, feeling stubborn all at once. "Maybe I won't have a household."

"Don't be foolish." Mama clicked her tongue impatiently. "Every girl gets married—or becomes an old spinster."

Well, Sadie thought grumpily, maybe she'd rather be an old spinster than married and running a household. But she held her tongue, not daring to say this out loud to her mother.

Cicadas hummed and the soft cooing of a pair of mourning doves floated into the kitchen on the dew fresh air. "It's a good day to do the bedding," Mama said, bending over the sink and looking up at the blue sky.

A good day to dangle hot feet in the stream, Sadie thought. Did Mama ever cool her feet or long to be outside free of chores?

"Amy! Laura!" Mrs. Wilson called. "We're washing the bed sheets today."

No, Sadie decided, Mama would never want such foolish things, then Sadie's eyes widened as she realized Mama hadn't said anything about her helping. She hunched over the washbasin, desperately wishing she was small. If she escaped Mama's notice she might be able sneak away.

"What about Sadie?" Laura asked primly, carefully walking through the kitchen with Grandma's full chamber pot.

"She's minding the baby and there's the cream to be churned," Sadie's mother said. She pumped water into the big kettle and set it on the stove to heat. "And when you're done that, Sadie, I noticed there were more weeds than beans in the garden, so you can see to clearing them out."

Laura and Amy carried the large, metal tub and

washboard from the back porch into the yard, then Laura herded Amy up the stairs to the bedrooms. Sadie listened to her sister's voice lecturing Amy all the way. Miss Prim and Proper with her fussy ways and grown-up airs, Sadie thought irritably. Just because she was oldest, Laura thought she could boss everyone. She gave the plate a final, angry swipe and dropped it with a clatter onto the drying rack. She'd like to see Laura soaking in Mama's big washtub along with the bedding.

Alone in the kitchen, Sadie dried her hands and crossed to Lizzie's cradle. She lightly stroked the sleeping baby's plump, pink cheek, then tiptoed to the bottom of the stairs. She could hear her mother turning the mattress in Grandma's bedroom and Laura chattering a blue streak, so knew she was safe for a few minutes. She crept to the tiny room tucked away behind the kitchen—Arthur's room.

A narrow, iron bed had a sheet stretched neatly over it and a blanket folded on the end. Sadie thumped the mattress with one hand. It felt hard and lumpy and she thought of her own soft feather tick mattress upstairs. But then she had to sleep with Laura so maybe a hard, unshared bed would be better than a soft, shared one.

She looked swiftly around the room. A white nightshirt hung from a nail driven in the wall and the navy jacket from another. The room looked bare and too ordinary for someone from far away. Hadn't he brought *anything* interesting from England?

Dropping to her knees, Sadie raised the edge of the cotton sheet and found the trunk and brown bag stored beneath the bed. She stared at the bag a moment. She shouldn't look, but...the way Arthur had held onto it so tightly, there had to be something important in it.

Quickly, she dragged the bag out. Nervous fingers fumbled with its metal buckles and finally unfastened them. Plunging a hand inside, Sadie groped about, but could feel only two small objects at the bottom of the bag. She lifted one out and found herself holding a small, black-bound Bible which she tossed onto the bed. One Bible was pretty much like the other, and she saw plenty of those at Sunday services. Her hand searched again and this time pulled out a photograph. Sadie carried it to the small window and peered at it closely.

In the picture, Arthur stood beside a tall, thin woman. His mother, Sadie supposed. Even through the photograph's brown shadows Sadie could see the weariness and strain in the woman's face. But still, she looked pleasant, her hand resting gently on Arthur's shoulder.

"You get out of that room, Sadie Wilson," Grandma called.

Sadie froze. She had been looking at the photograph so hard she hadn't heard her grandmother come into the kitchen. Maybe if she kept quiet, Grandma would think she was mistaken and go away.

Sadie rapidly shoved the picture and Bible back in

Arthur's bag and pushed it under the bed. She stood still a long moment listening, but couldn't hear any sound from the kitchen. Maybe Grandma had left. She peeked around the door frame and looked right into the old woman's red-rimmed eyes.

"You shouldn't be at that boy's things," Grandma scolded her. "He's not got much, but what he's got is his own. He doesn't need a nosy girl poking about."

Cheeks red with shame, Sadie hurried across the kitchen to the sink and picked up the basin of dirty dishwater. Pushing the screened door open with her hip, she went down the steps to the garden and dumped the water.

She straightened up then, listening. The cows were bawling loudly, upset, but by what? Suddenly, Arthur ran around the side of the barn, leapt over the garden's straight green rows, and bounded out of sight.

Sadie's mouth fell open. She quickly dropped the basin and went in search of him. She found him cowering behind the shed.

"What are you staring at?" he asked sullenly as Sadie stood looking at him.

Color flared in Sadie's cheeks. He was right. She had been rudely staring, though she hadn't meant to. It was just...she was trying to find the riffraff in him. Trying to find something that showed he was a thief. There was nothing. To look at he was no different from anyone else. It didn't show his having no parents or home, but she couldn't very well tell him that.

"I was just wondering what you're running from,"

she said finally, crossing her fingers behind her back so the lie wouldn't count.

"The cows. Your father told me to take them to the field, but the beasts wouldn't go." Arthur's slim chest heaved in and out. "I waved a stick at them to get them moving you see, and they came after me. I thought they were going to bite me, so I ran."

Sadie frowned. It was the most she had ever heard him speak and she had to listen hard to make sense of what he said. The words were the same ones she used, but they sounded strange; his *As* and *Os* bent different from her way of speaking them. But, she decided, she rather liked his voice rising and falling as he spoke—kind of like singing. But what was he talking about? The cows chasing and biting him?

Sadie started to laugh. She couldn't picture their fat, lazy cows running after anyone, let alone biting them. An angry, white spark glinted in the centre of Arthur's blue eyes and Sadie swallowed her giggles.

"Cows won't hurt you. A bull would, but not cows," she assured him. "You lead one out first and the others follow. That's how you get them moving. Don't you know that?"

"How would I be knowing that, then? I never saw a cow up close before," Arthur said. His voice squeaked higher. "There's no such beasts in the city."

Sadie plopped down beside him. She should get back and do her choring, but the baby was asleep and she'd only stay away a minute.

"What city?" she demanded.

Arthur's face suddenly froze and he squeezed his eyes half shut and peered at her. "What do you care? Didn't your mother say you weren't to have anything to do with the *Home boy?*" he added bitterly. "I might eat you!" He bared his teeth at her.

Sadie shrugged, not wanting him to see that she felt frightened and foolish all at once. She didn't know anything about this boy. Would he harm her? But she remained sitting beside him, confused as to why.

A kitten pranced out of the barn and tumbled headfirst into Arthur's lap. He laughed and gently stroked the tiny body.

"What city did you come from?" Sadie asked again. Watching Arthur's fingers tenderly rub the kitten's stomach had taken away her fear. There was no harm in Arthur.

"London, England," he answered shortly.

"We picked you up at the train station in London, but that was London, Canada," Sadie told him. "Is your London different from here?"

Arthur's eyes darted around the yard, then to the open fields beyond the farm. A shudder ran through his thin body.

"Very different," he said. "In my London there's buildings and always people about. There's too much space here. Makes a fellow nervous-like everything being empty like this." He gestured around the yard.

Sadie gaped at him in surprise. She liked the sky blue and wide above and the land stretching green and gold to the bush. Lately these open spaces had been the only place she felt she still fit. The rooms in the house had somehow become smaller and she was always bumping a hip on the table or tripping over a chair leg. Only when she ran fast in the open fields did her body belong to herself once more.

"London's huge. A grand city," Arthur said. "Not much green grows there. Our flat's in the bottom of the house, so it's always dark inside." His eyes had a faraway look. "The houses are all joined together in a row as far as you can see down the street. Always something going on, even at night. Carriages and people about..." His voice trailed off as he looked again at the expanse of fields in front of them.

People—that reminded Sadie of the picture in Arthur's room. "Is your family coming to Canada, too?" she asked.

"There's only Mum and me. Dad died shortly after I was born— typhoid it was. Mum was a schoolteacher until she took sick in her lungs. It was Mum who named me Arthur." His voice wobbled.

"After the king," Sadie said solemnly.

"Yes." Arthur got abruptly to his feet, eyes blinking rapidly. He strode across the barnyard scattering hens, ducks and geese. Sadie ran to keep up to him. "That's one ugly chicken," he said, pointing at a large bird.

Sadie clapped her hand over her mouth so he wouldn't see her lips quiver. "That's a turkey," she said quietly.

Arthur stopped and watched the large bird peck at the ground. "A turkey, you say."

"Yes," Sadie replied. "Come on. I'll show you how to get the cows to pasture."

It is very hard work in Canada. We are up at four or five o'clock every morning and we work hard all day. At night when we come in the house we feel very sleepy. We have to pay for everything we break that does not belong to us.

I remain, your Home boy,

S.G.

"Our Canadian Post"

St. Peter's Net, England, 1908

CHAPTER 5

Sadie hurried to put butter and bread on the table. She would not cry, she told herself sternly, but felt a tear slide down a slap-reddened cheek. Laura bustled from stove to table, a smug smile on her face that said she hadn't left the baby untended or the cream curdling in the summer heat. Amy sniffled, head cradled on her arms as if she'd been the one battered by Mama's angry words and furious slaps instead of Sadie.

Where had the time gone? She'd helped Arthur herd the cows to the flats near the stream, then shown him the back field where her father and the oldest Thompson boy, James, were cutting oats. On the way back to the house, she'd stopped by the pond to watch shiny-backed dragonflies darting above the water, admiring their expert dodging of long reaching frog tongues. Next thing she knew it was dinnertime and she'd had to run pell-mell across the fields to get home before Dad, and the cream hadn't been churned, nor had the garden been hoed.

The porch door suddenly banged open and Arthur came in carrying the rickety table from the barn that held the milking cans. Open-mouthed, the three girls watched as he placed it next to the stove then waited, shoulders rounded as if expecting a blow. Sadie stole a quick look at her mother. Mrs. Wilson's lips were tightly clamped together, the corners puckered as she stared at the table, but she said nothing, merely handed Arthur his plate.

James Thompson and Sadie's father came in, hair wet from a wash at the outside pump. Mr. Wilson raised his eyebrows at the sight of Arthur seated at the small table, but he too said nothing. Sadie's mother and Laura moved briskly from stove to table with bowls of vegetables and plates of meat.

Sadie watched Arthur at his table. "Mama. Why can't Arthur eat with us?"

Mrs. Wilson whirled about, eyes flashing. Sadie stepped back quickly. Watching Arthur bring in the table had made her forget Mama being mad at her.

"Because he's hired help and hired help does not sit with the family," Sadie's mother hissed. Apron fluttering angrily, face red, she looked like the old, fierce hen in the coop. The only thing keeping Mama's hands from slapping her again, Sadie knew, was James

Thompson sitting at their table. Mama would not want him going back home telling tales about their family. But he was hired help too—for the day at least—yet Mama let him sit at the table.

"Any of you girls seen the new harness I bought last week for the mare?" Mr. Wilson asked.

Amy, Laura and Sadie silently shook their heads. They knew better than to touch anything in the barn without their father's permission.

"Been misplaced, I guess," Mr. Wilson said. "Turn up some time."

"Mr. McMillan says he's having trouble with things being misplaced, too," James told them. "He thinks it's that Home boy he has that's the cause of it. He says the boy's light fingered. Wouldn't surprise me in the least. My Dad says those Home children should never have been allowed to come here. They're the offspring of criminals and drinkers and loose women…and they follow suit."

As Sadie watched her mother's face flushed red then suddenly turned white.

"Enough of that talk at the table," Sadie's father said.

"Sorry, Mrs. Wilson," James apologized.

Sadie stared at her mother. What had caused the sudden paling of her face? She already suspected part of the reason—the secret. The secret caused the blood to drain from her mother's face, caused her father to look concerned, caused her own stomach to quiver, though she didn't know why.

"Neither my father nor my mother were criminals or drunkards."

Sadie whipped her head around at the quiet words coming from the corner. Arthur stared at James Thompson a long moment, then calmly continued to eat.

"Just telling you what my Dad thinks about Home children," James muttered. "Isn't any need for them to be here."

"Your father has five sons," Mr. Wilson said mildly.

Sadie stole another look at Arthur and saw, despite his apparent calm, the hand holding the fork tremble.

After an uncomfortable silence, James cleared his throat.

"McMillan has a wonderful sorrel filly he's thinking of selling when it's grown. Chestnut brown."

"Saw her out in the pasture. Looks like she'll grow to be a fine animal," Mr. Wilson said.

"She'd be a beautiful sight pulling a buggy. What I wouldn't give to buy her myself if I had the money," James said. "Speaking of buggies, do you need a ride to Margaret McIntyre's picnic on Saturday, Laura?"

Laura turned pink. Sadie gawked at her. Why would James Thompson talking to her cause Laura to blush? Laura had hated James Thompson ever since the day he'd whipped up her skirt and shown the schoolyard her underclothing. Laura had locked herself in the school outhouse and not come out the rest of the day. Sadie studied her sister. What had Laura done to her hair? Instead of braids, it was parted in the middle, brushed away from her face and coiled into a loose bun at the back, copying the way the older girls wore theirs. All for James Thompson?

Sadie eyed the boy sitting by Dad. Sixteen now, wide and solid, his hands twice as big as her own. Yet with his small, bead-like eyes set deep in his face, he reminded her of the sow.

"She won't be needing a ride because she's not going," Mrs. Wilson said. "Saturday's a working day. Some people may have time to gallivant around but not us."

"Well, on Sunday afternoon some of us are going to…" James began.

"Sunday is for going to services and visiting family," Mrs. Wilson interrupted.

Laura meekly lowered her head, but Sadie noticed her sister's fingers steadily crumbling her bread.

~~~

Arthur's head nodded over his small table, the red flush of long, hot work slowly draining from his face, leaving it grey. Wanting to take advantage of the good weather, Sadie's father and Arthur had worked long into the evening, stooking the cut grain and drawing in dried barley until darkness forced them to stop.

"Boy's exhausted," Grandma grumbled.

"He'll toughen up soon enough," Mr. Wilson said.

"Or die in the trying," Grandma retorted.

"Boy, fill the troughs for the cows," Sadie's father growled.

Arthur forced his eyes open and slowly crossed to the back door. His feet were shuffling just like Grandma's, Sadie thought as the door shut slowly behind him, as if it too were tired from the effort of opening and closing all day.

"Sadie," Grandma said. "Run upstairs and get my liniment for my knees, that's a good girl."

Wanted her out of the kitchen, Sadie decided as she went up the steps. She could hear Laura and Amy in their bedroom, Laura sharp and impatient with the small girl's slow buttoning of her nightdress. Laura might find her own nightgown hard to fasten tonight Sadie thought, especially if all the buttons were cut off.

She circled around Grandma Wilson's bed, wrinkling her nose at the room's odor. It smelled like dusty, old thistles, not exactly a bad stink, but not a particularly pleasant one either.

Voices drifted up from the kitchen and Sadie quickly dropped to her knees and pressed her ear to the opening.

"You're working that boy too hard, Thomas," Grandma protested. "He's not very strong yet."

"Worked harder than him at the same age," Sadie's father said.

"And who's to say you weren't worked too hard. Doesn't make it right," Grandma pointed out.

"Leave the running of the farm to me."

Sadie heard the stamp of her father's feet as he crossed the floor, then the angry slam of the door.

"Takes better care of the horses than that boy," Grandma muttered.

"The boy is hired help," Sadie's mother said. "Besides which, a Home child should be grateful for any food and shelter given him. He could be out on the streets."

"Don't get high and mighty with me, girl." Sadie heard her grandmother's voice sharp with anger. "It's a short memory you have. A little kindness never hurt anyone and you, of all people, should know that."

All at once Sadie felt the secret leave its hiding place and flow up the stovepipe ready for her to hear. She quickly squirmed away from the hole and sat hugging her knees. Did she really want to know the secret? Once heard, she could never not know it. Was she brave enough to know the secret? She heard the metal clang of a pot bottom slammed hard against the stove top and leaned forward to listen.

"That aunt of yours—the way she treated you," Grandma said. "You did not pour drink down your father's throat. You did not make your father leave his wife and child and you did not cause your mother to die and leave you to be taken in by a wicked old woman who only gave you shame and nothing else. You were a child, left alone in the world—like that boy out there—and there's no fault to you or shame in that. Shame belongs to the people who can't see it that way, who can't show kindness."

"I do not want to discuss it," Sadie's mother said.

Sadie heard the runners of Grandma's rocking chair drumming furiously on the floor. "Not talking about something, doesn't make it go away."

Sadie climbed to her feet, feeling her legs wobble beneath her. Mama was an orphan—like Arthur! Taken in by an aunt. She hadn't thought about it before, but only Wilson aunts and uncles and cousins came visiting Sundays. Mama never said anything about her family. She had kept it a secret—and now— Sadie had to keep it a secret too. A secret that settled heavily around her heart.

Sadie found the liniment on Grandma's dresser, then sat on the side of the bed holding it. She felt like she had the time she'd fallen from the hay loft and bumped her head—like nothing she saw or felt was real. She glanced over at the hole in Grandma's floor. It was quiet now, but still she'd wait here a while for the anger to drain out of the kitchen.

We were nearly all sick on board the ship, and for two or three days we could not eat anything at all....Directly we left the ship we went in the train straight to Montreal, and then we arrived at the place where we were to stop....The next day the people came to fetch us.

Your affectionately,
C.M.
"Canadian Corner",
St. Peter's Net, England, *1905*

"The Home Visitor said the boy should be going to school until he's turned fourteen," Sadie's mother announced.

Sadie dipped hot water from the warming tank on top of the stove and poured it over the soap shavings in the dish pan. What was the point of being named after a king if everyone called you *the boy*.

"Read and write, boy?" Sadie's father asked.

"Yes, sir," Arthur said, eyes suddenly watchful and anxious.

"Won't be wanting to go to school then, will you?"

"Yes I would, sir. I promised my mother I'd get an education. And...and I like books."

"Hmph," Sadie's father grunted. "Like books...Have

to keep up your chores though, school or no school."
He pushed back his chair, stood and stretched. "Our
duty to send him if he wants to go, Aggie," Mr. Wilson
continued. "Have to wait a while, though. Apples need
to be picked and packed. Hospital in London wants
some barrels. Last of the oats should be drawn in too
while it's dry. Noticed the sun's got a ring around it
this morning so we can expect rain in the next couple
of days. Guess I can spare you about mid-October to
start school."

A smile lighting his face, Arthur headed for the back
door. He stopped a moment by Lizzie's high chair and
gently tapped the baby's hand. Glancing up, he caught
Mrs. Wilson's icy look, and immediately stepped back
from the baby, the smile sliding from his face. He
turned and went out.

"Sadie," Grandma said suddenly. "Run upstairs and
you'll find a book inside the top drawer of my dresser.
Bring it down for me."

Sadie stole a look at her mother, quickly dried her
hands and ran up the stairs. In Grandma Wilson's bedroom, she glanced at the stovepipe hole, then quickly
looked away. She hadn't listened there since the
evening she'd heard Mama's secret—a secret that now
left her miserable and uncomfortable when around
her mother. Mostly though, she feared meeting
Mama's eyes, frightened Mama would find the knowledge of the secret there. Yet other times she found herself intently studying her mother, trying to see this
new Mama who was an orphan. It was so confusing.

48

Not talking about something doesn't make it go away, Grandma had told Mama, but Sadie knew she'd never be able to speak to her mother about the secret.

She opened the dresser drawer and rummaged around until she found the book. Pulling it out she leafed through the yellow, brittle pages. It was an old school Reciter, good to start the fire with, but that was about all. She ran back down and dropped the book into Grandma's lap.

Her grandmother waved her away. "Put it on Arthur's bed, near his pillow so he sees it."

"Why?" Sadie asked.

"Oh, I know it doesn't look like much," Grandma said, "but when a person likes books it doesn't matter what shape they're in. It's the smell and feel and the words printed on a page that's important. Now do as I say and put that book on his bed, then straight out again."

Sadie slowly walked into Arthur's room. He actually wanted to go to school. Her own stomach churned with the thought of classes starting. Mr. Dawson cracking his wooden pointer on her desk, making her hands sweat and her heart pound. Seemed like yesterday summer had stretched endlessly before her. Now, suddenly, it was over and it was the first day of school.

She tossed the book on Arthur's bed. Books! Imagine. He liked books! Books were something to be feared. Pages full of words her tongue stumbled over as she stood trembling in front of the class trying to shape and force them into speech.

Sadie's eyes darted curiously around Arthur's room. Not much had changed since she'd been there last, except Arthur had wedged a board between the window sill and wall to make a shelf and had set his mother's picture on it. His sick mother. What would she think of Arthur being their hired help? Sadie quickly went back into the kitchen.

"Now Sadie, I want you to hold Amy's hand on the way there and back. It's her first day at school." Mrs. Wilson set two silver lunch pails on the table. "Are you listening to me?"

"Yes, Mama." Sadie avoided her mother's eyes and grabbed the two pails.

"I'll tell you if Sadie doesn't take care of Amy, Mama," Laura promised as they started down the lane toward the main road. Sadie stuck her tongue out at her older sister. Laura, she saw, no longer wore a pinafore over her dress and her hair was pulled back and coiled at her neck instead of being braided. Thought she was all grown-up now.

"Laura," Sadie called. "There's a spider walking up your back."

"I don't believe you." Laura flounced ahead.

"It's black and hairy," Sadie continued. "It's climbing toward your neck."

Laura shrieked and began to slap at her dress.

"I don't see anything, Sadie," Amy said softly.

"You don't?" Sadie's eyebrows rose, disappearing into her hair. "Guess I was mistaken."

Sighing deeply, she dragged her feet, covering the

toes of her boots with fine brown dust. Autumn, the best and most interesting time of the year—apples ripening, trees bursting with color, the threshers coming—and she had to go to school. Why did it seem like the days inside the schoolroom had more hours in them than those out?

"Sadie, you're squeezing too tight," Amy complained.

Sadie relaxed sweaty fingers. Already she could feel the sun's heat on her back, though the ditches still held wisps of white night mist. It was going to be one of those hot, late September days. She scratched legs made itchy by wool stockings. Mama had them wrapped up like it was the middle of winter, insisting they wear stockings and boots so they appeared proper.

They passed Arthur in the orchard near the road, high on a ladder tugging on apples. He stopped for a moment to watch them, his thin figure looking wistful, as if, Sadie thought, he envied them going to school. Well, he could have the books and the learning. She wanted nothing to do with musty words and baffling numbers.

~~~

Sadie raced down the lane dragging a tear-stained Amy behind her. The small girl had cried most of the day, unsettled by the boisterous boys and Mr. Dawson's wooden pointer. They ran through the orchard, but

Dad and Arthur were no longer there, so Sadie raced on to the back field.

Mr. Wilson stood on top of a large mound of oats piled high on a slow moving wagon spreading out the bundles that Arthur and James Thompson tossed up with long pitchforks. Sadie ran alongside them.

"Guess what, Arthur? I found England on the map at school. It's small." She waited expectantly for his surprise at this news, but Arthur merely nodded. "Canada is much, much bigger," she said and again waited, but still Arthur said nothing. She remembered then the wide expanse of blue between England and Canada. The ocean. It would take forever to cross.

"England's very far away, isn't it? Did you like the ride on the ship?" she asked.

"I was mostly sick," Arthur replied shortly. His shoulders sagged and his arms trembled as he grunted and raised the fork heavy with a large bundle of oats.

"Are you ever going back?"

Arthur walked to the next stook. "Mum got sick, you see. She couldn't work any more and we didn't have the rent money for the flat. There was only my Mum's sister, my aunt to take us in, but she has eight children of her own, so Mum took me to the boy's home and agreed to let them send me over here. I could've taken care of her. I could've got a job and kept us." He stabbed his fork into the stook. "She made me go. The Home told her I'd get an education here. Canada would give me a future if something should happen to her. Made it sound all wonderful going to a new country. She'll send for me if she gets better...when she gets better."

"No chores, girl?" Mr. Wilson's voice thundered from atop the piled oats.

Sadie grabbed Amy's hand and ran toward the house.

This woman told him that the child was from a home and "you know as a general thing all these children are liars."

Report of Mr. H.B. Willing,
Keystone Newspaper, published in
St. Peter's Net, England, 1905

It was like walking through an enchanted world. Each leaf not yet fallen, every blade of grass not brown and wilted, wore a coat of white. Like icing on Mama's Special Day cakes, Sadie thought. There had been a hard frost last night. She heard Arthur's footsteps following behind on the road. It was the first day Sadie's father had been able to spare him from the farm to go to school.

"Amy, you walk with Laura." Sadie pushed the small girl ahead. Still scared of school, Amy was forever clinging to Sadie's hand or skirts and at times Sadie found her closeness suffocating. She turned and waited for Arthur to catch up. He shivered in his thin, navy jacket.

"It's beautiful out here," he said, gazing about, his face looking more alive than Sadie had ever seen it.

"It's hoarfrost," Sadie told him. "Pretty, isn't it?"

"Wonderful. What makes it, then?" Arthur asked.

"It's the water in the air freezing, Dad says."

"Too bad it's so cold," Arthur complained.

Cold! Sadie stared at him. How would he feel when he had to wade through snow piled up past his knees to get to school? She liked drawing the sharp air through her lips, feeling it ache her teeth and burn her throat, but warming up before reaching her stomach. She liked too the way the white frost floated around her in soft feathers from the trees above, when touched by the sun's melting rays. But none of that mattered now. She had been waiting impatiently to have a further talk with Arthur.

"Who's the king you're named after?"

"You don't know about King Arthur?"

Sadie felt dumb, then mad that he made her feel that way, but swallowed her anger. She'd never find out anything if she got yelling at him. "Only what Grandma said about his being from Cornwall and having knights," Sadie replied.

"He was a king of England a long time ago, though most people believe he was only a legend," Arthur said.

"A legend?" Sadie repeated.

"A legend's like a story, something made up, you see. But me, I believe he was real. King Arthur was a great warrior, the best there'd ever been," Arthur told her.

"He'd a wonderful sword, given to him by a lady who lived in a lake. Made especially for him because he was king. It had precious jewels on it and shone brighter than any other sword ever known. And it was magic."

Sadie's eyes widened. She could see plain as plain the jewelled sword held high in a king's hand—shining—but she didn't quite know about a lady living in a lake.

"He was kind of like me, King Arthur was," Arthur continued. "No one knew for sure who his family was so some people said he was no good and shouldn't be king. But he proved himself, and his knights, they believed in him, and he became king."

"Sadie." Amy had returned, tugging at Sadie's sleeve. "Laura won't let me walk with her." She sniffled softly.

"Laura!" Sadie yelled. "Take Amy's hand."

"No!" Laura shouted back. "It's all sticky and she keeps grabbing my dress and wrinkling it. I'm trying to keep it nice looking for school. Besides mother said you were to take care of her, not me."

Sadie started up the road toward Laura.

"Never mind her," Arthur said.

Sadie stopped, but stood glaring at her sister.

Arthur smiled down at Amy. "Would you walk with me then? I don't often get to hold hands with a beautiful lady."

Amy giggled and stretched out her hand to Arthur. Sadie watched, liking the way Arthur spoke gently to the small girl. He just seemed to know that Amy couldn't take a person talking loud to her. She stared at Amy's hand now clasped in Arthur's and a sudden pain hurt her chest and the thought flitted through her mind that it might be nice to hold Arthur's hand herself. Instantly, Sadie felt her face burning hot. She rubbed a hand across her forehead. First a pain, then a fever. She must be coming down sick with something!

Arthur and Amy came up beside her and Sadie lowered her head not wanting him to notice her red face.

"What magic could the sword do?" she asked quickly, then added, "At the fair last year in London, I saw a man pull an egg out of Laura's ear. Right out of it, and I know there wasn't an egg there before." It suddenly mattered that Arthur not think she was dumb through and through. She wanted him to know that she knew about magic.

Arthur laughed and Sadie glared at him suspiciously, then smiled, too. It wasn't a laugh aimed at hurting her.

"Eggs are pretty good magic," he said. "But the sword's magic was better. It could heal King Arthur's wounds as fast as he got them. One minute a sword would be stuck in him, blood pouring out everywhere and the next minute he'd be all better and ready to fight again." He nodded his head, pleased as if he himself had been responsible for the sword's magic.

Amy's mouth rounded in surprise, while Sadie's dropped open. That was good magic. Much better than having an egg pulled from your ear.

"But the best thing about King Arthur was that he was very brave. Even when things went bad, he was brave—and kind." Arthur hesitated a moment, then added shyly. "My Mum would tell me stories about King Arthur most nights before bed. Said she wondered how I could sleep after hearing such frightful tales."

Sadie's chest ached again. She could see plain as plain Arthur tucked in his bed and his mother, the lady in the photograph, telling him stories in a gentle voice. How he must hate living in her house, where there was no storytelling or gentleness.

Arthur swung Amy's hand high, making the small girl smile happily. "There's stories of King Arthur written down in books," he told Sadie. "If I had enough money, I'd buy one."

Sadie frowned. Buy a book? Seemed like a waste of good money to her.

"Is this your new boyfriend?"

Sadie's head jerked up. She had been listening so hard to Arthur she hadn't notice their arrival at the yellow brick schoolhouse. Edith Morrison stood blocking the path, smiling prettily at Arthur. She was a half cousin of the Wilsons and her father owned the mill. Seeing Edith's dainty hands and feet, it seemed to Sadie her own suddenly grew three inches. Hair braided neat and sensible that morning became plain and dull next to Edith's golden curls, and her own muddy brown eyes couldn't hold a candle to Edith's wide, blue ones. Sadie felt a clumsy, ugly giant next to the girl.

"He's our Home boy," Laura announced.

"Laura, be quiet," Sadie hissed. She felt warmth

flood her face, as all at once she was embarrassed to be seen with Arthur.

"Your Home boy!" Edith exclaimed. The bright smile vanished from her face. "You're walking with a Home child?"

"She's not supposed to," Laura told her. "Mama did say she was to have nothing to do with him. But Sadie never listens."

"Laura," Sadie warned.

"We don't even know who his family is," Laura continued. "Mama didn't want to take him in, but Dad needed help with the farm."

"My father says Home children are trash," Edith said. Ice blue eyes swept over Arthur. "Pulled from the gutters. He says you have to keep an eye on them else they'll steal you blind or," she paused a long moment, then continued, "kill you while you sleep."

Sadie glanced at Arthur. His face wore its now familiar locked away look. Where did he go when he got that look? Somewhere where words wouldn't hurt him? She wouldn't mind knowing a place like that. But it bothered her that Arthur went away from them more and more often. What if some day he didn't come back?

The school bell rang and Edith began running toward the yellow building. Sadie hurried after her. Their teacher, Mr. Dawson, did not *tolerate tardiness*. She flung her coat onto its peg and slid into her seat, carefully avoiding the spot where the wood had cracked. She had sat one whole morning with a splinter sticking painfully in her thigh, but couldn't get it out without squirming and Mr. Dawson did not *tolerate fidgeting*.

Arthur stood at the back of the schoolroom as the children filed in and seated themselves. Amy was in the front row with the other beginning students. Sadie sat in the middle, though Mr. Dawson often threatened to send her up to the front, and Laura was seated one row behind with the seniors. Mr. Dawson slammed his pointer across his desk and the room instantly stilled.

"You are a new student?" Mr. Dawson asked Arthur.

Arthur nodded his head.

"And your name?"

"Arthur, sir. Arthur Fellowes."

Sadie whipped her head around to look at Arthur. Strange, but she hadn't thought of Arthur having a last name. Though that was silly, everyone had a last name. A snort of laughter, quickly muffled, came from behind her. Someone must, Sadie decided, think Arthur a funny name like her Dad had done.

"Your year of birth?"

"1901, sir."

"And where are you residing?"

"With the Wilsons," Arthur replied.

"Well, Arthur Fellowes." Mr. Dawson handed Arthur a senior reader. "Please read from page sixty-one, and we'll see what level you have achieved. You are able to read?"

Suddenly, Sadie hated the sound of Mr. Dawson's

shrill, high voice. Funny too but she hadn't noticed before how short Mr. Dawson was, and how he kept his head tilted back so his nose waved high in the air. To make himself seem taller, Sadie realized. A quick glance at Arthur's face told Sadie that he didn't much like Mr. Dawson either.

Arthur flipped through the pages, then began to read.

As I saw the last blue line of my native land fade away like a cloud in the horizon, it seemed as if I had closed one volume of the world and its concerns, and had time for meditation, before I opened another.

Sadie sat stunned. The words poured from Arthur and she was drowning in them.

…to gaze upon the piles of golden clouds just peering above the horizon; fancy them some fairy realms, and people them with a creation of my own.

Each word fell like a single, crystal waterdrop filling an emptiness in Sadie she hadn't even been aware existed. Once she had found a clear, pink stone in the creek. Running her fingers over its smooth sides and seeing it sparkle in the sun had filled her with a fierce joy. The same joy she felt now.

Arthur read better than anyone else in school. In fact, Sadie looked triumphantly at Mr. Dawson—even better than the teacher. Snickers grew into whoops of laughter as Arthur read. Sadie looked around the class-room puzzled. What were they laughing at? Why didn't Mr. Dawson yell *silence* and bang his pointer on a desk?

"Doesn't he talk funny?" Edith leaned over and dug her elbow into Sadie's side.

Sadie had become so used to Arthur's way of speaking that she had forgotten how strange it had sounded at first. Edith continued staring at her, eyes expectant, and Sadie suddenly knew why. If she laughed at Arthur with the rest of the class, Edith would be her friend; would welcome her into the small circle of older girls that huddled together in the playground. If she didn't laugh, no one in the whole school would talk to her. Sadie would be on her own.

Sadie's stomach tightened. After a long moment, she forced a small, choked giggle from between stiff lips and Edith sat back in her seat smiling happily at her. Sadie thought she was going to be sick. She wanted to get up and run far away, but she couldn't. She had to stay sitting in the schoolroom.

Arthur's face turned beet red, but he continued to the end of the page.

"Well, I see you can read," Mr. Dawson said, mouth pinched and sour. "I hope your mathematics are up to the same standards. You may seat yourself at the back with the senior students. I expect you will soon lose that unfortunate accent and learn to speak properly."

Sadie sat the rest of the long day hating Mr. Dawson and Edith and mostly—herself.

Canada wants increased population, but she would not on that account thank any country for landing the inmates of its prisons and poor-houses on her shores. The criminal, the diseased, the pauperized and the vicious are not wanted.

"The Importation of Waifs",
The Globe, Toronto, Ontario,
October 9, 1884

CHAPTER 8

"Some of the money's missing." Mrs. Wilson turned from the cupboard, holding the jam pot that she used for keeping the egg and butter money.

"Sure you didn't miscount?" Mr. Wilson asked. He ran a finger around the collar of his Sunday shirt easing its pinching at his neck.

"I didn't miscount," Sadie's mother said sharply. "There was $4.35 in here ten days ago and now there's $1.85."

Sadie stopped pushing Lizzie's arm through the sleeve of her coat and looked up at her mother, dread knotting her stomach.

"Spent it and forgot," said Sadie's father. He flicked open his pocket watch, studied the hands for a few minutes then snapped it shut and pushed it into his pocket.

"I haven't had the pot out since the last time you

went to town nearly two weeks ago, and I know there was $4.35 in it then." She held out a handful of coins. "This is all that's left now."

Her mother tilted her head and Sadie followed her gaze out the window to where Arthur was hitching the horses to the wagon, readying them for church.

"It's that boy," Mrs. Wilson said. "He's stolen the money—money meant for the church missions. It's wicked."

"What money?" Grandma Wilson came into the kitchen breathing heavily from coming down the stairs. Laura followed, having helped her grandmother dress for church.

"Mama thinks Arthur stole the butter money," Sadie said.

"It was meant for the church missions," Amy added. Her bottom lip trembled, the tension in the room upsetting her.

"You don't know Arthur took that money," Grandma Wilson protested. "With everybody helping out with the threshing this week, people were in and out of the house all the time."

"Those people are our neighbors—Mr. McMillan, the Thompsons, and the McIntyres," Sadie's mother exclaimed. "They wouldn't steal from us. What a suggestion!"

"All I can say," Grandma Wilson continued, "is that you don't always know people as well as you think you do. Why don't you just ask Arthur? Solve the problem quickly."

"What's the point of that. He'd just deny it. Home children have no sense of right from wrong." Mrs. Wilson clucked her tongue impatiently. "Very well. Ask him."

Mr. Wilson called out the door and a moment later Arthur came into the kitchen, his eyes growing anxious as he glanced from face to face. Sadie's mother slammed the jam pot on the table, the loud bang making Amy jump. Lizzie began to cry. "What do you have to say for yourself?" Mrs. Wilson said.

Arthur looked bewildered. "I don't know what you mean."

"Did you take the money that was in the pot, boy?" Sadie's father asked.

"No sir," Arthur replied.

"There." Mrs. Wilson threw up her hands. "I told you he'd say that. Doesn't know right from wrong."

"I didn't take the money," Arthur insisted.

"Of course he took the money. No one else here would. How can you sit in church this morning? A thief!"

Mr. Wilson sighed deeply. "You better stay home from services today, boy, until we can get to the bottom of this. Bit of choring you can do in the barn while we're gone."

Arthur's face looked stunned like someone had slapped him, then suddenly blankness smoothed away the distress like a mask settling over his face. "Yes, sir," he said.

Sadie finished buttoning Lizzie's coat, then scooped

up the baby and held her close, suddenly needing the comfort of the small, warm body. Why wouldn't Mama believe Arthur? Just because he was an orphan? Mama had been an orphan, too, and no one would ever think her a thief.

"Guess I'll stay home, too," Grandma Wilson said wearily. "Don't feel much like going to church any more."

Sadie didn't feel much like prayers and hymns either, but one look at Mama's face sent her hurrying to the wagon.

~~~

Sadie finished clearing the dinner table, then checked that the lamps were topped with oil and trimmed for lighting that evening. She looked around the kitchen searching for something—anything to do so she could put off as long as possible joining the company on the porch.

After a cool start the day had become unseasonably warm for late October. Indian summer Dad called it. Edith and her parents had come back to dinner after church. Mr. Morrison and her father had gone for a ride in Mr. Morrison's automobile with Patches running behind trying to bite the car's tires. Mama, Amy and Laura had carried out chairs to the porch for Edith and her mother to sit.

Sadie stood just out of sight behind the screened door, watching a wasp drunk on sun-drenched air throw itself against the screen. She heard Mrs. Morrison recount an endless list of Edith's accomplishments, which she finally exhausted only to have Edith continue with her own list of achievements.

"Shall we make ice cream?" Sadie heard her mother say quickly when Edith paused for breath, and Sadie knew Mama was finding the visit a strain, too. Chairs scraped on the porch floor. Sadie stepped back and decided she couldn't listen another minute to Edith and her mother. She ran through the parlor, out the front door and headed for the barn. At least the animals could hold their tongues.

She pushed open the heavy barn door and quickly pulled it shut behind her. It took a moment for her eyes to adjust to the gloom.

"Arthur," Sadie called softly. She'd been worried all afternoon because Arthur hadn't come to the house for dinner.

Old Bob raised his head and watched as she peered into the shadowy corners of the stalls then climbed the ladder to the loft and found Arthur lying in the middle of a family of kittens who climbed all over him. He didn't seem to notice, but stared unblinking out the window in the loft where the hay was brought in. He didn't take his eyes away from the opening even when Sadie sat down beside him.

"Do you see that bird up there circling," Arthur said. He took a hand from under his head to point out the window.

Sadie looked out and saw a lone bird gliding in

wide circles above the flaming reds and yellows of the maple bush.

"That hawk?"

Arthur shrugged. "Hawk, whatever it's called. Flying wherever it wants. I wish I was that bird," he said. "Up there, free."

Sadie frowned. "What do you mean—free?"

"Free to choose. I never had a choice. I was just put on a ship and sent to this farm. No one asked me if I wanted to go—I was just sent. And now I have to stay," he said bitterly. "Your father has signed papers that say I have to stay for a whole year and if I leave before the year is up, I get put in jail."

"Jail!" Sadie exclaimed.

"That's what the Home told me. If I tried to run away I could be put in jail. Mind you," Arthur added with a bitter laugh, "your mother wants to put me there anyway thinking I stole her money. Thinks just because I don't have a family, I'm a criminal—a thief. Everyone thinks all Home children are that."

Sadie picked up a piece of straw and began to shred it.

"Do you think I stole that money?" Arthur propped himself up on his elbows and looked directly at her.

Sadie felt her cheeks grow hot and kept her eyes on the straw being whittled away beneath her nervous fingers. She didn't know what to say. Could a person want to be free so bad they'd steal? Could she say no and keep her fingers crossed behind her back because she wasn't really sure? But that didn't feel right.

After a long, silent moment Arthur turned back to the window. Feeling uncomfortable and awkward, Sadie scrambled to her feet. Heading to the ladder, her foot hit something solid. She reached down and picked up the reciter Grandma had given Arthur.

"Were you reading this?" she asked.

Arthur didn't answer.

Sadie turned the pages. "Why do you like books so much?"

Arthur raised himself into a sitting position and wrapped his arms around his knees. "Do you remember asking me how it felt on the ship and I said I was sick mostly..."

Sadie nodded.

"What made me sick was the deck moving all the time, never still, and the fear of knowing there was nothing beneath me but deep, black water. Well, that's how it feels to me here..." He gestured around the loft. "...like I'm still on that ship and there's nothing steady or solid under me. Reading helps take that feeling away—at least for a while. When there are words in front of me, a story being told—I'm not so scared."

Sadie handed him the book and made her way down the ladder. At the last rung she paused, looking up into the shadowy recesses of the loft before stepping off the ladder. She stopped and stroked the old dog's head. "What do you think, Old Bob? Did he steal the money?" she whispered.

She gave the dog's ear a farewell tug, then walked slowly out of the barn and across the yard.

"I tried to save you some ice cream," a small voice said at her elbow.

Sadie looked down and saw Amy holding a dish of white, sticky liquid. "Put it down for the cats," she said. "A treat for them."

"Where were you?" Laura asked. She and Edith sat on the bottom step of the porch, shawls wrapped around their shoulders. Sadie shivered as a chill wind swirled leaves about her feet and blew across her arms raising goosebumps. Indian summer was over.

She began to push past the girls to make her way up the steps, when Edith reached up and plucked a piece of straw from the back of Sadie's dress. "She's been hiding in the barn," Edith said, holding up her prize. "There's hay all over her back. Does your Home boy stay in the barn?" she asked slyly.

"Edith! That's an awful thing to say," Laura hissed, glancing nervously at the porch door. She jumped to her feet and began to sweep the straw from Sadie's dress, in hard, angry strokes.

"I didn't mean it like that," Edith said sulkily. "She's so big and ugly no boy, Home child or otherwise, would ever look at her anyway."

Laura let go of Sadie's skirt and advanced on Edith. "Sadie isn't ugly," she said, bending over a cowering Edith. "She has beautiful brown eyes and when the rest of her grows and catches up to her arms and legs, Edith Morrison, she'll outshine you." She pointed a finger at Edith. "I'm warning you. You say one word at school about this and I'll tell everyone you're smitten with our Home boy. I'll tell them there was straw on *your* back."

Edith gasped, eyes wide with disbelief, then got to her feet and flounced up the porch steps into the kitchen.

"Thank you," Sadie said uncertainly. Laura thought she had beautiful eyes?

Laura turned on Sadie, face flushed with anger. "Oh, you won't be thanking me once I tell Mama," she spat. "She told you to keep away from that boy. You should be ashamed of yourself. The only reason I said those things was to keep Edith from telling the whole school that my sister is a shameless hussy. I wouldn't be able to hold my head up. So don't be thanking me."

She flew up the porch steps and the door banged shut behind her.

The fellow who owned the place...he was a doctor. I was up on the wagon, they pitched hay up and one guy was careless and he reached too far and stuck the tine of a fork right into my thigh. I was laid up over a week....Not once did that doctor come up and see me...No one put a poultice on it, or bandaged it. Nobody cared.

John Atterbury,
Surviving Home child

CHAPTER 9

Sadie sighed and poked her toe into a clump of soggy, brown leaves. She wished the dinner break would end. She never thought she would actually want to go back into the schoolhouse, but even lessons and Mr. Dawson's droning voice would be better than Edith's constant chatter of dresses and boys. She looked around the schoolyard. The ground had grown hard with November cold, the trees stripped bare. Low black clouds scuttled across the sky. Watching them, Sadie wished it would snow, hoping the white might take away some of the grey she felt.

She saw Arthur standing alone, huddled against the schoolhouse wall, his thin jacket pulled tight against the wind. Grandma wondered each day when the Home Visitor would come and bring him a heavier coat. Sadie looked quickly away when she saw him raise his head. She didn't want him noticing her watching or worse, catching her eye.

She hadn't talked to him in two weeks, since Laura had complained to Mama about Sadie walking to school with the Home boy. How it shamed her to see Sadie with him. But unexpectedly, Laura had said nothing about the hay on Sadie's dress. Now, Mama kept her so busy in the mornings with chores she had to run to school to get there before the bell rang. There was no time for talk with anyone.

"Sadie, are you listening?" Edith stood with her hands on her hips, glaring at her.

Sadie sighed deeply and turned back to the group of girls, and knew plain as plain she would keep listening to Edith every dinner break, because it meant being included, not left out. Like Arthur.

She stole another look from the corner of her eye and this time saw a group of boys sauntering toward him, led by the Thompson brothers. Alarm swept through her. James and Albert were too old to attend school this year, but that still left three Thompson brothers to make trouble.

"Guttersnipe!" one of them jeered.

"Limey."

"Bastard!"

The word rang clear in the cold air. The girls gasped and the smaller children quit their game of tag to watch. Suddenly, a hand reached out and slammed Arthur against the wall. Another flicked his hat high into the air and a foot ground it into the dirt.

"Well, what else would you expect from a Home child," Edith sniffed. "Fighting like dogs in the street."

"Those other boys started it," Sadie protested weakly, trailing off as Edith glared at her.

She saw Arthur's arm draw back, his fist meet a nose and red spurt down a coat front. Then she could see nothing but flailing arms and feet. It was unfair of them ganging up on Arthur. Movement at one of the school windows caught her eye and Sadie looked up to see Mr. Dawson watching the boys, but he made no move to stop the fight.

Suddenly, Sadie heard a man's voice shouting and saw her father wade into the brawl. He emerged dragging Arthur by the back of his coat. Mr. Wilson glanced up at the school window and Mr. Dawson quickly stepped back out of view, but Sadie knew by the scowl on her father's face that he had seen the teacher.

Arthur's hands remained tightly clenched as he gasped for breath, then all at once his body sagged and his arms hung limp. He had no fight left in him. Amy walked over and picked Arthur's hat up from the ground and held it out to him. Arthur started to snatch it away, saw who was holding it, and took it gently, tiredly nodding his head at Amy. Watching, Sadie felt tears sting her eyes. She should have been the one to give him his hat—to show the others in the schoolyard that she didn't care what they thought about Arthur. But it hadn't been her—it had been Amy.

The circle of boys fell back uneasily as Mr. Wilson swung around to look at them. "Need all of you to take on one boy?"

No one answered.

"Hmph..." Mr. Wilson looked around the schoolyard and back at the window. "Sadie, Amy, Laura. Get in the wagon."

"But Father," Laura began. "School's not over yet."

"The wagon!" Mr. Wilson thundered.

Amy sniffled all the way home, as if she had been the one caught fighting. Laura sat with her back stiff, pointedly ignoring Arthur, but his head never surfaced from his hands so he didn't notice. With a teeth-banging jolt over the frozen lane, Sadie's father pulled the wagon into the yard.

Mrs. Wilson ran from the kitchen, pulling her sweater tight across her chest against the cold. "What's happened? Why are they all home?"

"Boy's been in a fight. Outnumbered six to one and that sap Dawson watching," Sadie's father said. "Decided to bring them all back. Fool teacher can't keep order."

"I knew it," Sadie's mother cried. "I knew that boy would be trouble. He's a bad influence. What will people think of us having such a boy? He should never have come to stay."

Without a word, Arthur jumped down from the wagon and crossed to the pump. He worked the handle up and down and pushed his head beneath the thin stream of water that poured out the spout. Watching him, Sadie wondered if her mother was right. Before Arthur's arrival, life had been well-ordered and running smoothly. Dad hadn't minded having all girls and she hadn't heard Mama's secret. Arthur had come and her world turned upside down. Like their being home in the middle of a school day.

Arthur had said that he felt like he was on the deck of a ship, unsteady with nothing solid beneath. Well, that was how she felt right now and it was all Arthur's doing.

Suddenly Sadie felt very tired. She knew deep down there was no point in blaming Arthur. Things would have changed whether Arthur was there or not.

"They said awful things to him, Mama. Called him names," Sadie said.

"One boy said a swear word," Amy added.

Sadie's mother stared at the small girl in surprise. "Did you hear her? You see the shame he is bringing to us," she said to Sadie's father. She turned back to the girls. "Get into the house. All of you. If you're going to be home, you may as well make yourselves useful. Sadie, there's some apples need paring for drying. Laura, you mix up some pastry." Sadie's mother flapped her apron at them, like they were hens she was shooing into their coop. "Amy, I'd like you to explain how you know what a swear word is."

"Thompson boy had a bloody nose." Sadie heard her father say before the kitchen door slammed.

After supper that night, Sadie sat at the kitchen table, her mouth silently shaping the words in her school reader. She had thought about Arthur's mother telling him stories every night. Well, Mama was too tired and busy to read to Sadie. So she had decided, if she wanted to hear stories she would have to tell them to herself. But first she'd have to learn to read.

So every night for the past two weeks Sadie had practised, and each passing day found her able to string the words together more and more easily. Finally came a wonderful moment, when she could hear the story through the words.

A gust of wind threw hard pellets of snow rattling against the kitchen window. Grandma pulled her chair nearer the stove.

"Cold goes right into my bones," she said. "First snow of the year."

She smiled at Arthur, who huddled next to the stove, looking miserable. He had a cut above one eye, and a swollen lip, but worse, his nose had begun dripping and his eyes shone brilliant blue with fever.

Grandma studied him for a long moment, then picked up her knitting. "Read us something, Sadie," she said.

Sadie felt pleased. She liked reading aloud. Liked the comfort that stole into the kitchen with the words. Mama's face would soften as she bent over her mending, though that could be the dim lamplight. Dad's farm paper would fall into his lap, and Amy would sit still to listen. Even the baby quieted. Only Laura ignored her, turning the pages of the Timothy Eaton catalogue, sighing over the waists and skirts.

Sadie looked through her reader and found a poem she thought Grandma would like. She read the words over first inside her head to get used to them, then out loud. She wished the words flowed from her mouth the way they did from Arthur's, but her tongue still stumbled at times.

Snow

This is the way the snow comes down,
Softly, softly falling;
So God giveth the snow like wool,
Fair and white and beautiful.
This is the way the snow comes down,
Softly, softly falling.

Sadie finished reading and sat a moment enjoying the echoes of the verse that lingered in the kitchen. She glanced up to see Arthur smiling at her. Sadie felt hot and cold all at the same time, yet happier than she had in a long while. It took her a moment to figure out why, then she knew. Arthur's smile said that he understood why she had laughed with the others, why she didn't walk to school with him or talk to him. She had been forgiven, in fact, had never really been blamed. The only one making her feel bad was herself. Sadie's mouth stretched in a wide grin.

Mrs. Wilson raised her head from her sock darning and looked sharply from Sadie to Arthur. "Boy, that woodbox needs filling for the morning," she said.

"Yes Ma'am," Arthur replied. He threaded his arms into his jacket and pushed open the porch door. The cold air bent him double in a spasm of coughing as he went out.

"You've got plenty wood. There was no call to send the boy out tonight. Anyone with eyes can see he's not well," Grandma said.

"I'll run my own household, thank you, Mother Wilson," Sadie's mother answered shortly.

Grandma thrust her knitting into the basket. "Sadie, where's the big stone?" she asked.

Sadie went into the back porch and found the large, white rock the size of a loaf of bread. The sick stone. In the winter the irons stayed permanently on the warming shelf of the stove ready to wrap and put into their beds each night to take the chill off the sheets. But whenever someone in the family was ill, Sadie's mother would heat the sick stone on top of the stove, wrap it in towels and warm the sickbed. The stone held heat much longer than the irons. Sadie liked pushing the towelling aside and rubbing cold feet over the stone's warm, rough surface, enjoying its solid comfort.

"Put it on the stove to heat up," Grandma ordered.

Sadie hesitated, unsure what to do. Her mother's darning needle flashed silver as she angrily stabbed it in and out of the wool sock, but she said nothing so Sadie did as Grandma asked.

"People call themselves Christian...go to church...uppity now, forgetting who they are." Grandma's knitting needles clacked furiously, the rocking chair runners thumping crossly on the floor.

Sadie felt the secret creep into the kitchen and swirl about the stove, woken by Grandma's words. Words spoken that hid more than they said and words weren't supposed to do that.

"I'll help the boy," Mr. Wilson said.

Sadie could tell he was anxious to escape the kitchen and the secret and so was she. Noiselessly she left the kitchen and went upstairs. Better be like Dad and leave before her mother could find something to get mad at her about.

Shivering in the cold, still air of their bedroom, Sadie wriggled into her nightgown and slipped into bed, groaning as bare feet slid through icy sheets. In her haste she'd forgotten to bring up an iron.

She lay listening to the clunk of wood being dropped in the box and the sounds of Arthur coughing. Why did her mother dislike him so much? There were people Sadie didn't like, such as Edith, but that was because Edith was bossy and overly fond of her own voice. But her mother didn't even know Arthur. She didn't like him just because he was a Home child and that didn't seem much of a reason at all.

She heard Arthur cough again and rolled over onto her side pulling the quilt up over her ears, trying to breathe warm air into the bed. When she was sick Mama made her soup and carried it upstairs. A cool hand would feel her forehead, then tuck the blankets in tight about her. It made it almost worthwhile to get ill so you could bask in that warm, cared-for feeling. The woman in the photograph, Arthur's mother, looked like she would make you feel cared for, too.

Sadie suddenly sat up. Who was going to wrap the sick stone in a towel and put it into Arthur's bed? It was too heavy for Grandma and Sadie knew for certain neither her mother nor father would do it. She lay back down. Arthur would have to do it himself.

I never saw the inside of a house for three months. Ate in the woodshed, slept in the woodshed; worked from daylight 'til dark....My name was never mentioned, I was always called "the boy."

Cosmo DeClerq,
Surviving Home child

CHAPTER 10

"They're here, Mama," Amy cried from her post near the window.

"So soon," Sadie's mother exclaimed. She surveyed the kitchen table full of platters of meat and bowls of vegetables, whirled about and counted the pies. "Sadie, run downstairs and bring up some peach and pear preserves, just in case the pie doesn't go around."

Sadie ran down into the basement to the shelves that held row after row of jars of pears, peaches, plums and other fruit. In the dim light coming from the top of the stairs, she stood happily looking at the endless supply of vegetables and fruit Mama had put down for winter, enjoying the secure feeling they gave her. They'd not go hungry this winter.

"Sadie, quickly now." Mama's cross voice floated down to the basement.

Sadie grabbed two jars and ran up the stairs into the kitchen. The room was crowded with men, neighbors come to help at her father's buzz saw bee, cutting the wood that would see them through the next winter. Working together, the men had cut the Thompson's wood first, then her Dad's and next in turn was the McIntyres. They brought with them the odors of wet wool, sour sweat and new snow to mingle with the hot kitchen smells of pie crust, apple cider and roasting meat.

Suddenly shy, Sadie lowered her head and pushed her way to the far side of the kitchen to where Amy had squeezed herself tightly into the corner by the parlor door.

Mr. Wilson strode past them, opened the door to the parlor and set his watch on the mantle above the fireplace. "Forgot to take this out of my pocket when I went for the mail earlier," he said, closing the door after him. "Don't want to lose it in the snow."

With much chair scraping and deep voiced laughter, the men seated themselves around the table until only Arthur stood alone, uncertain whether or not to sit with them. Finally, Grandma Wilson pressed him into a chair at the large table as she passed with a stack of thick sliced bread. "Doing a man's work," she said. "You sit with the men."

Seeing him at the kitchen table, Sadie's mother frowned, then became too busy keeping up with the men's appetites to bother with him. Laura and Sadie scurried about filling cups with hot cider and tea. Mrs. Wilson watched with satisfaction as bowls emptied and platters piled high with chicken, pork and beef were reduced to scraps. No one could say she didn't lay a good table.

"Best apple pie I ever tasted, Mrs. Wilson," Mr. McIntyre said, pushing away his plate and patting his ample stomach.

"My Laura made that," Sadie's mother said proudly.

Sadie watched her sister flush with pleasure, then saw her suddenly steal a glance at James Thompson from the corner of her eye. Probably hoping he'd heard the compliment. What Laura saw in him, Sadie couldn't imagine.

Pipes were lit and cups of tea drained as the men sat and talked letting their dinner settle, then confusion reigned once again as they milled about pulling on coats and boots. Then abruptly they were gone, leaving behind windows streaming water from the combined heat of bodies and a hot stove. They also left a table littered with dirty dishes.

Sadie's mother shook her head at the remains of the meal, then sighed deeply. "You girls start clearing up," she said. "I have to change Lizzie, then I'll be back down."

Sadie reached for the first plate and scraped bits of gristle and fat into a pail for the pigs' supper. "Did you see the way Laura was looking at James Thompson?" she said to Amy. "Big eyes," Sadie fluttered her lids. "Like she was in love with him."

Amy giggled.

"Why do you have to be so mean, Sadie Wilson?" Laura turned on her furiously.

"Because James Thompson is a pig. Pig eyes, fat pig body, he even eats like a messy pig. I can't believe you like him."

"Well, at least I like someone who comes from a good family, while you…you moon over a Home boy, someone who's not even good enough to eat at the table with us. Someday James will have his own farm," Laura went on. "It'd be nice to have my own house, fix it up pretty, keep it that way."

You'd marry James Thompson to have a house?" Sadie shrieked.

"Yes, I would," Laura screeched back. "To get away from you. You're such a spoiled brat. Dad's girl. You get to go to town, I have to mind the baby. If it's too hot inside, you hoe the garden, while I stay in making bread, pies, standing over a boiling kettle stirring preserves. Every morning I take out Grandma's slops and change Lizzie. I have to be Mama's helper because Mama says you aren't responsible enough. I can't even go out to a dance or a picnic—" Laura suddenly burst into tears and ran up the stairs.

Sadie stared at the empty spot where her sister had stood. It wasn't true what Laura said. They all worked hard. But…did Laura work the hardest, being the oldest? Sadie thought guiltily of all the times she'd slipped into the barn or down by the pond to escape chores.

She handed Amy a cloth. "I'll wash and you can dry," she said. Hands soaking in the warm, soapy water, she stared out the window above the sink. Clouds hugged the ground and the wind whistled about the house, pushing snow and sleet before it. Occasionally she caught a glimpse of a sledge through the swirling grey curtain, as it headed toward the house from the bush with a load of cut wood. Was James Thompson driving it? Change, she realized, would have come whether Arthur stayed with them or not. The kitchen darkened.

"I'll have to light the lamps," Sadie's mother said, coming into the room carrying Lizzie. Grandma Wilson followed slowly behind. "It gets dark so early these days. And Amy, for heaven's sakes, close the door to the parlor. Who on earth left it open, letting the cold in here," she exclaimed. She plopped Lizzie in her high chair, then crossed to the stove, lifted a lid and lowered a long taper into the flames.

"James Thompson," Amy whispered pulling the parlor door shut.

"What?" Sadie said.

"James Thompson left the parlor door open," Amy repeated.

"Don't be so silly," Mrs. Wilson said. "What would James Thompson be doing in the parlor." She poured drippings from the crock sitting on the stove into the large, black frying pan and sliced ham into it. "Just finish cleaning up dinner and its time to make supper." She looked around the room. "Where's Laura?"

"She had a bad headache, Mama. She's gone upstairs to lie down," Sadie said absently, thinking about what Amy had said.

"Very well. Sadie, let Amy and Grandma finish those pots. You peel the potatoes and make sure there's some left when you're done."

Sadie dumped potatoes into a basin and crossed to the pump to wash them. Passing Amy she heard her whisper, "He really did."

Sadie stopped to stare at her, but Amy didn't notice, intent on drying a fork. Grandma Wilson, Sadie saw, also stared at the small girl.

Fat sizzled and the smell of frying potatoes and onions filled the kitchen as Mr. Wilson pushed open the porch door. "Turning real nasty out," he said, unwinding an ice-caked scarf from around his neck and hanging it on a hook.

Sadie glanced out the window and in the storm's dim grey light saw Arthur leading the horses to the barn to rub them down.

"Glad to get that job done," Sadie's father said. "Final load we cut has to be stacked in the shed but that's all that's left to do. Arthur can finish tomorrow." He stood a moment near the stove thawing his fingers, then crossed to the parlor and pushed open the door.

Sadie shivered at the sudden rush of cold air that flooded through the open door to collide with the kitchen's heat. Mr. Wilson stepped back into the kitchen pulling the parlor door firmly shut behind him. "You put my watch away, Aggie?" he asked.

Sadie's mother shook her head. "Either of you girls touch Dad's watch?"

Sadie and Amy shook their heads.

"Mother?" Sadie's father raised his eyebrows at Grandma Wilson.

"I've not been near the parlor," she said.

"Didn't sprout legs and walk off," Mr Wilson said. "Someone took it."

"That boy," Sadie's mother said. "That Home child."

"You're awful quick to blame him," Grandma Wilson said.

"Harry McMillan sent back his Home boy because he was stealing from him," Sadie's mother pointed out.

"That's his Home boy, not ours. Besides no one ever proved that boy stole a thing either."

"We can settle this once and for all," Mrs. Wilson began.

Sadie heard the door behind her open, felt the rush of cold air and smelled the strong barn odor that came in with Arthur.

"Search his room. See if the butter money is there, the harness, the watch…and who knows what else he's taken," Sadie's mother continued. "And if you find anything, he goes."

Sadie turned and saw Arthur staring at her mother, his face like stone. Without a word he turned and went back out. There was a long silence after he left, broken by Mrs. Wilson. "Searching his room is the only way we'll know for sure," she insisted.

"Terrible thing to do to the boy," Grandma Wilson said.

Memories of Arthur watching the hawk, speaking

softly to Amy and telling them with pride the story of King Arthur—King Arthur who was noble and good— came to Sadie. Mama was wrong. The knowledge hit her like a blow in the stomach. Her Mama could be wrong. Was wrong. Arthur hadn't stolen a thing and if Mama had taken the time to know Arthur, she would see that too.

"Amy said James Thompson was in the parlor," Sadie said shakily, aware Mama would be mad that she was being so outspoken.

Her mother crossed the room in quick, angry steps to stand in front of her. "James Thompson has no need of money or a watch," she said fiercely. "Why you take that orphan boy's side over your own family's I just don't know."

"Just because he's an orphan doesn't mean he steals," Sadie said desperately. "You're an orphan, Mama, and you don't steal."

The words were out of her mouth before she could stop them. Horrified, she watched the anger drain from her mother, leaving behind a grey-haired, tired shell of a woman.

"I'm sorry," Sadie said, listening as her words dropped into the sudden silence, sinking deeper and deeper.

I should like you to let me know whether my mother is alive, or if I have any friends I could write to.

I am, yours faithfully,

M.G.
"Our Canadian Post",
St. Peter's Net, England, 1911

Sadie jerked awake. Something had disturbed her—a sound. Body tense she lay listening, but all she heard was the wind howling around the eaves, piling snow in drifts against the side of the house. Trees moaned and creaked, rubbing their bare branches together. She kicked Laura's leg off her own, then burrowed deeper into the warmth beneath the quilt. Drowsily, her eyes began to close when she heard it again—a distinct though muffled thud.

This time, Sadie climbed out of bed and peered out the window, but couldn't see a thing through the white swirling snow. It didn't matter. She felt certain the sound had come from inside the house anyway. She hadn't been asleep long, she reasoned. Her muscles still had a heavy, tired feeling, so it couldn't be Dad and Arthur up for morning chores.

She quietly left the bedroom, glancing back to make sure Amy and Laura slept on. At the stairs she carefully placed her feet against the side of each step where it met the wall, so there'd be no telltale squeak to give her away as she crept down them. In the cold dark of the kitchen, she stood shivering, wishing she'd stayed in bed.

The room felt empty and frightening without her family to fill it. A sudden gust of wind rattled the porch door and Sadie's heart leapt in her chest. Then above the noise of its fierce beating she heard a soft thump—from Arthur's room.

She hopped from foot to foot on the icy floor, uncertain what to do. If Mama came down and found her standing there, she would skin her alive. But what if Arthur was sick and needed help. He'd never completely got over his cold, his nose still dripped. She'd just take a lightning-fast look, make sure everything was all right, then race back to bed.

She tiptoed through the kitchen to the door of Arthur's room. In the pale, eerie snow-light she saw him shoving shirts and pants into his brown bag. The photograph of the lady lay on the bed ready to go in on top. She gasped and Arthur swung around to face her.

"What are you doing?" Sadie asked. He was running away.

"I'm leaving," Arthur said. He turned back to his packing.

"Leaving? Leaving for where?" Sadie wrapped her

arms around herself, trembling violently from cold and fright. Thoughts churned in her head. If Mama found her here…Arthur was leaving…he'd brought so much change, but she didn't want him to go…she'd never hear any more stories of King Arthur…

"Back to England," Arthur said. He picked up the photograph, tucked it inside a pant leg, then fastened the bag's clasps. "I have to know if Mum's alive or dead." He hesitated a moment, then continued fiercely. "I hate it here. I want to go home."

He picked up the bag and pushed past Sadie into the kitchen. Sadie followed not knowing what to do. Should she call her father? Just let Arthur leave?

"It's storming awful bad tonight."

Sadie and Arthur both jumped. Grandma sat in her chair by the stove, a black, bulky shadow wrapped in a shawl. "You wouldn't get very far in this storm, especially being sick and all," Grandma went on. "And you, girl," she scolded, "young ladies do not go into gentlemen's bedrooms in the middle of the night."

Sadie's heart began its uncomfortable thudding again. Please don't let Mama find out, she prayed. If Mama didn't find out…Sadie's mind worked frantically…if Mama didn't find out, she'd never be mean to Laura again.

"Light the lamp and put the kettle on the stove, like a good girl," Grandma told her. She settled back in her chair. "We'll all have a cup of tea and talk this out, and then if Arthur still wants to go, we won't stop him."

Sadie let out a relieved breath. If Mama came down

now, Grandma would say she couldn't sleep and had asked Sadie to make her a hot drink. Except—Sadie suddenly frowned. Except, she'd already promised to be nice to Laura. But—she brightened a little as she filled the kettle—she hadn't said exactly for how long. She would be nice to Laura for a little while, then...well, she'd see.

She touched fire to the lamp's wick and golden light spilled into the kitchen. Arthur stood hesitantly, looking from Sadie to Grandma Wilson, then slowly lowered his bag to the floor. He opened the stove door and shoved in thin sticks of wood, poking and stirring until flames showed red and yellow. Sadie looked around in satisfaction. Gone was the dark and the fear. It felt like her kitchen again. She handed her grandmother and Arthur a cup of tea, and drew her chair close to the glow of the stove, cradling her own warm cup in her cold hands. She hoped Grandma would convince Arthur to stay.

"Why are you leaving, Arthur?" Grandma asked.

Sadie noticed that Grandma always called Arthur by his name. Never, *boy*, like her mother and father did.

"I need to know if my Mum's alive or dead," Arthur said flatly. His face crumpled and he lowered his head into his hands.

Sadie could hear him sniffling, but decided it probably was his cold. Boys didn't cry—did they?

"I want to go home. To England." Arthur's voice sounded thin, strained by his fingers. "It's terrible here. At first everyone laughed at me, called me names and I thought that was bad. But now, no one speaks to me and, well, that's worse."

Sadie squirmed in her chair, uncomfortably aware that she was one of the ones who didn't talk to him anymore.

"And Mrs. Wilson thinks I'm a thief. I tell her I'm not, but she doesn't believe me. Wants to search my room."

"I'm sorry for you, Arthur," Grandma said. "But don't let a pack of fools get the better of you. You're a smart boy and given time, you'll get along all right. But tell me, how were you planning to get to England?"

Sadie looked at Grandma in surprise. If this had been Mama, Arthur would be yelled at, called ungrateful and told he was too young to decide anything for himself. Grandma treated him like he was a grown man, someone able to make his own decisions.

"I thought to join the army," Arthur said. "I haven't any money for the boat fare, you see, so I was thinking..." He took a deep breath. "Mr. Wilson said soldiers were heading out every day to England and I thought I'd be a soldier and make my way home."

A soldier! Sadie's eyes widened; yet, upon thinking about it, being a soldier might be interesting. Seeing different places and all. But would she want to be far away from her family? Alone, like Arthur?

"Hmm..." Grandma said. "You're a bit young for soldiering, though I'm sure you could tell your age falsely and they'd be none the wiser," she added hastily.

Sadie gaped at Arthur's thin frame. Couldn't Grandma see him properly? He couldn't fool anyone into thinking he was older! She opened her mouth to point this out, but a fierce look from her grandmother snapped it shut without her saying a word.

"The army's a hard, hard life," Grandma went on. "I'm sure you're thinking it could be no harder than this, but it is."

They sat silently listening to the wind and snow and Sadie could tell her grandmother was mulling over the situation.

"I'll write to the Home," Grandma said. "Maybe they can find out about your mother. Then once we get word, that could be the time for you to choose whether to go or stay. But as I said, the deciding of that is up to you."

Arthur considered a moment, then nodded his head. "You'll ask for sure?"

"Give you my word," Grandma promised.

Arthur looked down at his cup. "I'll stay a while longer then. Until I've heard."

Sadie thought he looked somewhat relieved. He hadn't wanted to be a soldier that bad, she guessed.

"I didn't steal anything," Arthur said suddenly.

"I didn't for a moment believe you had and Sadie, she doesn't think you're a thief either. Told everyone so."

"You did?" Arthur asked Sadie and she nodded, feeling uneasy remembering how long it had taken her to believe him.

She wriggled to the edge of her chair. "Now that that's settled," she said, "can you tell a story about King Arthur and his magic sword? I'm not a bit tired."

"Sadie," Grandma protested. "Arthur's not feeling well, and besides, you should be in bed."

But Sadie could tell from the sudden flicker in Grandma's eyes that she wouldn't mind hearing a story herself.

Arthur laughed. "Shall I tell you about his knights then? The Knights of the Round Table?"

Sadie leaned forward eagerly.

"The men who fought for King Arthur," he began, "were called knights. But they had to earn that title, you see, acting very loyal and noble and doing good deeds that helped other people. When the king and the knights all got together to tell stories about battles or the good deeds they had done, they gathered about a huge, round table that filled an entire castle hall. You won't be believing me, but 180 knights could sit at it at one time."

Sadie's brown eyes grew large. She looked at the wooden, four-sided table that could seat her family, an uncle, an aunt and a cousin or two, but couldn't picture one that was so big that 180 knights could fit.

"But why was the table round?" she asked.

"Because," Arthur said, "by sitting in a circle, King Arthur believed no one person could think they were better than anyone else. All men were equal."

The wind tugged and pulled at the farmhouse, but the wood in the stove crackled and burned and the lamplight kept the storm at bay. As Arthur spoke, wooden walls turned to gray stone hung with colorful, woven tapestries. Dogs growled, women scolded, and children ran about, while men laughed and talked. Wasn't it a wonder, Sadie thought, what words could do. Tell her wonderful stories, make glorious pictures in her mind. Until Arthur had come, she'd never known the power of words.

The farm kitchen faded and became a grand hall filled with a large, round table and Sadie could see plain as plain sitting about it surrounded by his knights, a king with a magic sword who greatly resembled Arthur Fellowes.

Have you got any English history books, if so will you send me one? And have you any books about the South Africa war? I am greatly interested in those kinds of books.

I remain, yours faithfully,

T.S.

"Our Canadian Post"

St. Peter's Net, England, 1908

CHAPTER 12

Sadie pressed her hands against Mary Lou's side, warming them on the cow's solid body. She peered over the broad back to see Arthur forking manure from the horse stalls into a wheelbarrow. Laura was already seated on her stool, pail ready to begin the evening's milking. Amy poured the pigs' food into their trough. The chores were being done early because of the Christmas entertainment that evening.

"Are you sure you won't come to the school tonight, Arthur?" Sadie asked anxiously. "I'm reciting a poem. One I made up myself," she added shyly. Written it for him, but she wasn't about to tell Arthur that.

"I'm holding the star while she says her poem," Amy told him importantly.

He shook his head. For three days he had haunted the kitchen and barn, unspeaking, white face shutting them all out. Forever, Sadie feared. He'd been like this since the letter came telling him of his mother's death shortly after he'd sailed for Canada. Sadie knew the bag beneath the bed remained packed and worse, the photograph of his mother had never been replaced upon the shelf. Would Arthur stay or go?

She sighed and set a pail beneath Mary Lou. Tugging hard she soon had a steady, blue white stream flowing and fell into the comfortable rhythm of milking, leaving her mind free to wander. She felt so strange these days. Detached. People moved around and about her, yet she felt separate from them all. She was waiting—waiting for Arthur to make his decision.

"Arthur," Amy said solemnly. "You need the magic sword."

~~~

The schoolhouse looked different at night, Sadie thought as they pulled up in the cutter. Yellow light spilling from the windows made the building appear friendly and warm. Inside, the pine tree the students had decorated earlier that day seemed taller and fuller than Sadie remembered. She and Laura hurried to hang their coats in the cloakroom only to find their way blocked by Edith—surrounded by a group of admiring girls. She was smoothing the skirt of a new red velvet dress.

"We were going to order a dress from the catalogue," Edith told the girls. "But Mother said you couldn't be sure it'd fit so we made a special trip into London just to get my dress for tonight."

Sadie pushed past, half hoping to crush the velvet, or at least put a tiny crease into its sleek perfection. She had to admit, it was the most beautiful dress she'd ever seen, with wide skirts and a close fitting bodice topped with a white lace collar, but she wasn't about to tell Edith that.

"We had such a time getting it home, because velvet marks so easily, you know," Edith went on. "It was very dear, but mother insisted I get it. She said I looked like an angel in it."

Sadie gritted her teeth.

"I see you're wearing your usual Sunday blue dress," Edith said, watching Sadie shrug out of her coat.

Sadie looked down at herself, wondering if the faint line showed where her mother had let out the hem. Would everyone see when she stood up to recite her poem? It was the first time she'd ever written anything herself. She'd been so worried about getting the words right, she had not given a minute's thought to how she'd appear standing in front of everyone.

"You look perfectly fine," Laura said suddenly. She reached up and patted the bow on Sadie's head. "The blue ribbon sets off your hair beautifully. Red wouldn't look half as nice." She grinned and Sadie felt her stomach settle a bit. People would be listening to her words, not bothering about how she was dressed.

One by one the children went up to the front of the classroom, reciting, playing piano or singing. Sadie nervously pleated her skirt, waiting her turn.

"I spent hours ironing that," Laura said crossly, yanking Sadie's hand away. "Nobody will mind a let-down hem, but they will notice wrinkles."

Then suddenly it was her turn. Sadie walked to the front on shaking legs. Amy trailed behind holding a yellow star hung from a long pole. It dipped and dived above Sadie's head and she hoped fervently that Amy could hold it and not have it come crashing down on her.

"Miss Sadie Wilson will recite a poem she has written herself." Mr. Dawson left the front with a tiny bow, and Sadie took a deep breath.

"*Hope,*" she began. Her voice wobbled and the words stuck firmly in her throat. She stared out over the audience, seeing her neighbor's faces ruddy from the stove's heat, saw her mother and father watching anxiously, and Grandma Wilson smiling and nodding encouragement. Then standing at the back she saw him. Arthur. He must have walked all the way from the farm—come to hear her poem.

Sadie took a deep breath and began again.

> HOPE
> A star
> In the sky
> At night
> Is a guarding eye
> A searching light
> A comforting hand
> A glimmer of hope
> To a grieving man.

There was a moment's silence after she finished, then loud clapping filled the schoolroom. They must have liked it all right, Sadie thought happily.

Piling into the cutter at the end of the entertainment, Sadie stared up into a black night sky awash with silver stars. Red velvet dresses and let-down hems seemed somehow unimportant out here, leaving no room in Sadie's heart for anything but a bursting joy. She listened to the runners swish through snow made crisp by bitter cold. She glanced over at Arthur and her happiness faded. His face remained blank. She'd thought maybe her poem...but he'd withdrawn back to the place he went, where no one and nothing could touch him. Like a cloak settling about her shoulders, Sadie felt the old detachment fall upon her. Still waiting.

"Dad," Laura said, as they pulled into the yard. "There's a light moving by the barn."

Old Bob was howling and Patches barked wildly and threw himself against the shed door. Someone had locked them in.

"Who's there," Sadie's father yelled.

The light bounced up and down as a figure ran away from the barn. Arthur leaped from the cutter and chased after the light. Mr. Wilson jumped down and followed. Sadie heard a loud *Oomph!* saw the light flare brightly, then go out as it hit the ground. A few minutes later her father and Arthur came back to the cutter, James Thompson between them. Sadie took a quick glance at Laura to see her sister's mouth rounded in a shocked O.

In the kitchen, Mr. Wilson emptied a bag James was carrying and three dead hens spilled out onto the table. James shifted his feet nervously, but said nothing.

Sadie's father walked to the telephone hanging on the wall. He cranked the handle, then spoke into the mouthpiece. "Harold. Thomas Wilson here. Sorry to trouble you so late, but I think you should come over here right away. No...no...all fine. Still, I'd appreciate you coming over."

He hung up the receiver and crossed back to the table. "No point in letting the whole county know our business," he said.

They all knew how some people spent whole days sitting by the telephone listening in on their neighbor's calls. "Your father will be here soon, but while we're waiting you can tell me why you've been stealing from me."

"I wanted the horse," James mumbled.

"What horse?"

"The mare Mr. McMillan's got for sale."

"Paid you for the work you did for me. Paid you fairly."

"I know, but Mr. McMillan wants to sell the horse soon and I can't earn the money fast enough," James said. "I'm sorry."

"Sorry..." Mr. Wilson repeated. "Still have my watch?"

"Yes, sir."

"You know this boy's been taking the blame for what you did," Sadie's father said, pointing at Arthur.

James nodded miserably.

"Guess we'll just wait for your father, then." Mr. Wilson looked up and noticed the girls. "Off to bed. No reason for you to be standing around gawking."

Sadie followed a dazed Laura up the narrow stairs. Glancing back over her shoulder into the kitchen, she saw her mother staring first at James and then at Arthur, a bewildered expression on her face.

∾∾∾

Wrapped in a blanket Sadie watched from the bedroom window as the cutter holding James and his father pulled away from the house. She'd heard the steady rumble of voices from the kitchen, but had felt no desire to listen at the stovepipe. Despite his size and age, Sadie knew James would get a licking from his father. Mr. Thompson was well known to have a free and heavy hand. His sons often displayed their father's handiwork at school. James would be hurting for many days.

She heard her mother and father come up the stairs, then the bed in their room creak as they settled for the night. Blanket tucked tightly about her feet, Sadie waited for the house to quiet. She didn't think Laura was sleeping, but couldn't tell for sure as her sister laid on her side, facing the wall. After a little while, Sadie went downstairs.

Grandma sat before the stove like Sadie knew she would be. She hadn't heard the old woman's steps on the stairs.

"Are you unwell?" Sadie asked.

"No. No." Grandma Wilson assured her. "The older I get the less sleep I seem to need."

"Will Mama like Arthur now?"

"I don't know," Grandma said. "Some ideas get stuck inside a person's head and just won't leave."

"But Arthur wasn't the thief," Sadie exclaimed. "James was. Mama has to see that it had nothing to do with Arthur. She was an orphan, too, so why can't she understand?"

"I don't know that either," Grandma Wilson told her. "It's something you'll have to ask your mother. It's not my story to tell. Ask your mother—and soon. The more time goes by, the harder you'll find it to speak."

Sadie headed up the stairs. Ask her, Grandma had said. But Sadie doubted she'd ever find the right words to ask Mama.

Mary Brown, a girl of 12, was the only living person on the farm with Miss Findlay the last three months of the boy's life. She gave evidence which went to show that Miss Findlay had beaten him severely at different times, having used axe handles and broom handles in chastising him.

"The Barnardo Boy—Trial of Miss Findlay for Manslaughter"
The Daily Free Press, London, Ontario, December 15, 1895

CHAPTER 13

"Sadie!" Mrs. Wilson's voice cut through the fog in Sadie's mind. "Sadie, are you listening to me?"

"She's not paying attention, Mama," Laura said.

"Yes, I am," Sadie replied. A quick spark of anger completely cleared her head. She could see plain as plain a lump of cold snow melting down Laura's warm back.

"Stop it, you two," Mama scolded. She turned back to Sadie. "Now, I'm expecting you to take care of Grandma and the baby. We'll be back by dark, so have the meal ready for us. Put the vegetables on at six, then fry up the potatoes," she said rapidly. She anxiously looked around the kitchen. "I'm sure there's something I've forgotten...Laura, where are the hens and geese we dressed for sale in town?"

"Dad's packed them in the cutter, Mama," Laura said.

"And the eggs?"

"Everything's ready."

"Well, then, I guess we're off. Be good now, Sadie."

"Yes, Mama," Sadie said.

Mama looked younger, Sadie thought, the deep lines about her mouth smoothed out by the anticipation of the trip to town, the weariness lifted from her eyes. Mama was tired, Sadie suddenly realized; tired most of the time. And no wonder. From dawn to dusk, her mother was never still; always moving, always working. Maybe next summer she would take Mama to the river and show her how to dangle her feet in the water.

She watched out the window as her mother climbed into the cutter and Mr. Wilson tucked a rug around her legs. Bright Eyes, the mare, stood unmoving, puffing white clouds that clung to her long head in the cold, still air. Dawn spread thin, pink fingers across the sky, the colors deepening to explode into yellow light as the sun burst above the horizon. It was two days before Christmas and her mother and father, Laura and Amy were going to London.

Mr. Wilson snapped the reins and the mare strained forward. Sadie's eyes burned and watered from the sun's glare on the snow as she watched the cutter dwindle to a small, black speck, then disappear altogether. Only then did she turn and look around the kitchen. Mama wanted her to scrub the floor while everyone was gone. She set a bucket of water on the stove to warm and picked up the broom. It could have been her going to town, but she'd offered to stay and let Laura go instead. A good deed, she'd thought at the time, but now looking at the dirty floor she wasn't so sure.

As she swept, she felt the familiar listlessness of the last weeks settle into her body. Her arms moved in the proper sweeping motions, but she felt apart from them. She had gone back to waiting.

Arthur came in from the barn, went to his room and a moment later, left again, hugging his coat tight about him against the cold.

"That boy sure looks hungry," Grandma said. Her rocking chair sat permanently by the stove now that winter was here.

Sadie's eyes went to the empty doorway where Arthur had been. Hungry? Her mother gave him as much food as they all had. He didn't look starved. In fact, recently she thought he'd lost his all bones look and had began to fill out.

"Not hungry for food," Grandma said, correctly reading her mind. "Hungry for talk, people...caring."

"Do you think he'll stay, Grandma?" Sadie asked. It felt good to finally speak her fear aloud.

"I don't know," Grandma replied. She sighed and rested her knitting on her knees. "Probably not, if he gets too hungry."

Sadie took the pail from the stove, hitched her skirt up and got down on her knees. She wet the scrubbing brush and began scouring the floor in wide circles. How would it feel to have no one? No one to care one way or the other what happened to you, not even care if you lived or died. She shivered, feeling a chill creep up her spine and quickly reminded herself that she had Mama, Dad, Grandma, Amy, Lizzie and even Laura to care about her.

~~~

Late afternoon shadows stretched long across the yard. The baby lay sleeping in her cradle. Grandma's chin had fallen against her chest and Sadie could hear a rhythmic whistle that meant the old woman slept soundly.

She opened the stove door and poked in wood. It would soon be time to make supper. She lifted one of the round stove lids, set it aside and peered in to see if the flames had caught. Satisfied that the wood was burning well, Sadie placed the pan of drippings on the stove, ready for frying the potatoes once enough heat had built up. There was nothing more to do for a little while.

She glanced around the quiet kitchen, then suddenly grabbed her coat, opened the porch door and ran across the snow rutted yard to the barn. She had had enough of waiting.

Arthur was examining a much mended harness when Sadie pulled open the heavy, wooden barn door.

He looked up when she came in, but went back to his work without speaking.

"Have you decided?" Sadie blurted out.

Arthur's fingers ran carefully over the leather, feeling the joinings. "Not yet," he said finally.

Sadie badly wanted him to stay, but she couldn't think of a proper way to tell him that. Words—always she had trouble with words. She had thought reading was hard, but at least the words were there printed in black before her, but finding the proper words inside herself to ask someone to stay was much more difficult.

"Did I ever tell you about King Arthur's wife?" Arthur said suddenly. His voice sounded rusty, like he hadn't used it much lately. Sadie remembered Grandma saying Arthur was hungry for talk.

"Her name was Queen Guinevere," he continued.

Sadie sighed. *Guinevere*—the name floated off the tongue, light and airy, while Sadie—well, Sadie plopped off, hard and heavy.

"She was very beautiful," Arthur said. "So beautiful that even though she was Arthur's wife, Lancelot, his best knight, wanted to marry her, too."

Sadie grimaced. It was hard to imagine being so beautiful that two men wanted to marry you, when you yourself had mouse-brown hair, plain features and were big for your age.

"Like Edith," she said bitterly.

"Ppfff..." Arthur snorted. "She's pretty enough but surely you don't think her beautiful?"

Sadie shrugged.

"Beauty comes from inside a person," Arthur told her. "It was what was inside her that made Guinevere beautiful."

"For real?"

Arthur smiled. "For real."

So curly, blonde hair and blue eyes didn't always make a person beautiful. Sadie felt happiness flood warmly through her, hurting her with its intensity, but she didn't mind. It felt wonderful.

"This'll do, I guess." Arthur gave the harness a final inspection, stood up and pushed the barn door aside to hang it on the nails set in the wall behind. Reaching forward, he glanced out the door. The harness suddenly dropped from his hand and without a word he ran from the barn toward the house.

"What's wrong? What's the matter?" Sadie shouted after him.

She followed Arthur into the yard, then stopped, horror holding her feet fast. Black smoke boiled from the kitchen roof. Arthur ran up the porch steps and yanked open the back door. Thicker smoke poured out, swallowing him as he plunged into the house. He was soon back.

"Sadie!" he yelled. "Take the baby! Sadie!"

Sadie ran to the porch, coughing as smoke was sucked down her throat. She took the bundle that Arthur thrust at her and pulled back the blanket. Baby Lizzie's eyes were closed. Fearfully, she shoved a finger under the baby's nose, then began to sob as it came away moist and warm. Baby Lizzie was sleeping despite all the commotion.

Arthur reappeared, half-dragging, half-carrying Grandma Wilson. The old woman doubled over coughing but she managed to wave a hand at Arthur.

"I'm all right. I'm all right," she gasped. "Get the fire out. Near the stove. Save the house."

"Take them to the barn," Arthur shouted, seeing Sadie standing, shock not letting her think or act. "It's warm there." He ran to the pump in the yard and furiously worked the handle up and down until a steady stream poured into a pail. "Then come back and fill up anything you can find. Hurry!" He grabbed the overflowing bucket and rushed into the house.

Sadie quickly spread straw on the barn floor then lowered her grandmother onto it. She flung an old blanket about the woman's shoulders and laid the baby next to her, then ran to the pump. Filling pail after pail with water, she put them on the porch where they would quickly disappear into the smoke, then return empty. In a short while, Sadie noticed that the black smoke had turned white and thinned out, then vanished altogether.

Arthur plodded slowly down the porch steps and leaned wearily against the pump, his face streaked black. "It's out. It's not as bad as it looks. It was mostly smoke. Something on the stove had caught fire."

Sadie stared at the brimming pail she still held in her hand. In the water's mirror she saw herself lifting the stove lid aside, the red and yellow flames licking the wood in the round hole, and the pan of fat drippings set beside it ready to fry potatoes.

"I didn't put the lid back on," she whispered. Her hand flew to her mouth in horror. She stared at Arthur. "I didn't put the lid back on and I put the fat next to the open flames." She began to tremble.

"It's all right, then. It was just an accident," Arthur assured her. "Not done purposely."

The cutter burst into the yard, the horse sweating and blowing hard from running.

"We saw the smoke!" Mr. Wilson yelled. "What happened?"

"The baby!" Sadie's mother stumbled from the wagon. "Where's the baby?"

"She's fine, Mrs. Wilson," Arthur said. "She's in the barn with old Mrs. Wilson. They're both safe."

Sadie's mother ran into the barn and came out hugging the baby tightly to her with one hand, the other helping Grandma Wilson over the snow churned yard. "It's his fault!" she screamed. "I warned you not to have a Home child. He could have hurt the baby. He's to go! He's to go now! I won't have him here another minute!"

Sadie set the pail of water down. Her arms ached and trembled. No one knew who had caused the fire. No one except her and Arthur. She didn't want Mama's terrible anger turned on her. She didn't think she could stand Mama's voice cutting into her. She could say Arthur did it. Her mother would believe her over a Home child. Or better still, she would say nothing.

That way she wouldn't be outright lying.

She glanced up and saw Arthur's eyes, extremely blue in his smoke blackened face. A wave of anger swept through her. All his talk of brave knights and good deeds. Couldn't he see she was just plain Sadie Wilson, not brave, not kind or noble. If she told she'd done it, Mama might turn her out, make her leave and she would be an orphan child like him—and Mama—belonging to no one. Arthur's eyes were still on her face, then suddenly they slid to his feet, defeated. Except...Sadie thought...except he would always know the truth of her and she would always know the truth of her and she knew she couldn't live with that.

"I did it," Sadie muttered.

Mr. Wilson's head whipped around. "Speak up, girl."

"It was my fault." Sadie could barely breathe through her fear. "I left the fat on the stove. I was going to cook the potatoes, but I went to the barn and I forgot about it. It must have caught fire. Arthur got Grandma and the baby out safely and stopped the fire spreading. It had nothing to do with him. I'm so sorry."

Sadie looked about the yard at images that would be forever etched in her mind—Amy and Laura's frightened faces peering from the back of the cutter; black soot staining the white snow; Grandma grey with exhaustion; Dad's face stern and deeply lined; and Mama's eyes stretched wide with disbelief.

"Aggie," Mr. Wilson said. "Get the baby and Mother into the house. You'll have to go in the front way. Sadie, go to bed. I don't want to see a hair of your head until tomorrow."

Mrs. Wilson started toward the front of the house holding Lizzie in her arms, losing her footing on a patch of ice.

"I could take the baby for you, Ma'am," Arthur said quietly. For a moment it looked like Sadie's mother would refuse, then abruptly she handed Lizzie into his outstretched arms. "Thank you, Arthur."

Sadie trailed behind her mother and Grandma Wilson through the seldom used front door and up the stairs. She undressed, shivering in the cold air, and crawled into bed. Everything stunk like greasy smoke. She buried her face into the pillow, but even there she couldn't escape the smell. She couldn't even cry she felt so numb. Couldn't even remember certain details any more. Except one. Mama had called Arthur by name.

Would you send me some mistletoe with berries on it if it's no bother to you? I should be very thankful to you if you'll send me a root of it, as it would be nice to have it growing here. I wish you and all the boys a Merry Christmas and a Happy New Year.

G.P.

"Our Canadian Letter Bag"
St. Peter's Net, *England, 1908*

CHAPTER 14

Christmas morning Sadie wakened to see a round bulb at the bottom of the stocking that hung on the end of her bed. Her Christmas orange. Her eyes misted over and she gulped back a sob.

"Are you crying again?" Laura asked in disgust. "That's all you've done for two days. It's a wonder you have any water left in you." Laura snatched her stocking from the opposite bedpost, turned it upside down and shook it.

"I didn't think I'd get anything this year," Sadie sniffled.

Laura was examining new mittens and red striped candy, no longer interested in Sadie's tears. For someone who thought she was so grown-up, Laura certainly emptied her stocking quickly enough. Sadie opened her mouth to point this out, then suddenly shut it, remembering. The night of the fire Laura had eased herself carefully into the bed beside Sadie, reached out and held her sister's hand. Sadie had clung to it all through that awful night.

Amy padded over from her small bed and crawled in beside Sadie.

"Santa doesn't mind that you burnt the house down," she said. "He knows you didn't mean to."

"I just scorched the wall behind the stove, Amy."

But it might as well had been the whole house. She and her mother had scrubbed every square inch of it, walls, floors and furniture to get rid of the black, greasy soot. It had been an exhausting job. By the end of the day her arms felt ready to fall off with tiredness, but Sadie hadn't minded. Cleaning had helped to take away some of the horror she'd felt. Mama and Dad hadn't punished her, saying the fright she'd received was punishment enough. Thinking about that, Sadie quickly pulled on her clothes. Mama could do with help on Christmas morning.

She burst into the kitchen to find her mother standing by the stove, and her father putting on his barn coat and boots, like they had every morning of Sadie's life. Seeing them there, tears brimmed up in Sadie's eyes.

"Thank you for not sending me away," she sobbed.

Her mother turned from the stove to stare at her. "What on earth are you talking about? Sending you away?"

"I almost didn't tell you I'd caused the fire because

I was scared you'd send me away and I'd be a Home child, like Arthur," Sadie cried.

Sadie's mother slowly lowered herself into a chair. She bent her head to stare at her hands twisting restlessly in her lap, unused to sitting idle.

"You could have got another boy like Dad wants," Sadie told them.

"Another boy!" her mother exclaimed. "Such foolishness. Where ever do you get such ideas?"

Sadie's eyes wandered toward the stovepipe leading to Grandma's room. Seeing where she looked, Mr. Wilson shook his head slowly.

"Used that myself when I was young," he said. "Trouble listening through a pipe is you don't always hear things properly."

Sadie hung her head ready to be scolded for yet another wrongdoing, eavesdropping. But Mama surprised her by not saying a word.

"Have the prettiest, smartest girls in the county," Mr. Wilson said gruffly. "Way you take to reading...writing that poem. Couldn't ask for better."

Sadie's mouth dropped open. She'd never heard Dad say anything flowery like that before.

"Mama," she began timidly. "Tell me about you being an orphan."

Amy clattered down the stairs and into the kitchen. Laura followed helping Grandma Wilson.

"Goodness, the breakfast is burning." Sadie's mother shot out of her chair and hurried to the stove. "Stir the oatmeal please, Sadie," she said over her shoulder and Sadie knew her mother wasn't going to tell her about being an orphan.

As Sadie stirred the porridge, she looked around the kitchen. The only reminder of the fire now was the unpainted boards behind the stove. With Arthur helping, her father had replaced the wall between the kitchen and Arthur's room. The fire had somehow burnt away the uneasiness between them, but not, Sadie knew, with her mother.

Arthur came from his room and plucked his coat from the hook. Sadie had a sudden vision of her own full Christmas stocking and saw plain as plain his empty bedpost.

"Before you go, Arthur," Grandma waved him over to her chair, reached into her knitting bag and handed him a brown, wool sweater. "Canadian winters are much colder than England's," she said. "I remember well my first winter here. Thought my blood would freeze in my veins. I hope it fits and all."

Arthur smiled taking the sweater being pushed into his hands. It had been a long time since she'd seen him smile, Sadie thought.

"Happy Christmas to you," Grandma said. "Don't you have something to give Sadie?" she suddenly added.

Mr. Wilson stopped on his way out the door and Sadie's mother turned abruptly from the stove. Amy and Laura stared first at Arthur, then at Sadie. Arthur's face turned red and he went into his room. Sadie could feel her own cheeks burning now, and wished they'd all stop staring at her like she'd grown a second head or extra arm. Arthur returned to the kitchen carrying a pile of papers. He crossed to Sadie and shoved them at her.

"This is for you, then," he said. "Your Grandma helped."

Sadie stared down at the papers in her hand. They were tied together on one side with brown wool, matching Arthur's new sweater, but in her confusion, she couldn't make any sense of them.

Amy stretched on tiptoe to see. "He's made you a book, Sadie," she said.

Sadie saw that Amy was right. Tied like that the papers did make a book. She turned it over and saw printing—*The Stories of King Arthur*, and beneath that *To Sadie Wilson from Arthur Fellowes*. Her name. Her very own name on a book made especially for her. Sadie didn't know where to put her eyes.

"Thank you," she stammered. Desperately, she tried to think of something else to say. Words! They made her so mad! She could never find the right words when she wanted them! But Arthur grinned shyly at her and she decided she'd done all right.

"Cows don't know it's Christmas," Arthur said briskly and strode to the door.

He sounded an awful lot like Dad, Sadie thought, as she listened to Arthur and her father stomp down the porch steps.

"Sadie's got a boyfriend," Laura whispered to Amy.

"I like Arthur," Amy said.

Sadie's mother pulled the curtain aside and watched the boy and man cross the yard, her mouth turned down in a worried frown.

"No harm in the boy giving her a Christmas present," Grandma said.

Sadie's mother sighed. "It's just..." She seemed at a loss to finish.

"Don't worry," Grandma reassured her. "She's got a lot of growing to do yet."

Sadie flipped through her book, stopping when she came to a story about a Guinevere with brown braids. No one had ever given her a present as wonderful as this before. But—her happiness faded—she had no gift for Arthur.

Sadie thought hard all Christmas day. She thought about what Grandma had said, that Arthur was hungry but not for food. She felt again the incredible joy Arthur's reading had brought her and how she now loved words. She remembered Arthur, soot-stained and choking, handing her the baby and going back into the burning kitchen for Grandma. She thought about the knights sitting at the round table in King Arthur's castle none better than the other, and she thought about the book Arthur had made for her, with the story of a tall, big-for-her-age, brown-haired Guinevere.

"Sadie," her mother called, breaking into Sadie's thoughts. "Set the table for dinner."

Absently, she lined up the forks and knives, setting places for her mother and father, Amy, Laura,

Grandma Wilson and herself. Suddenly she stood very still, staring at the table, then quietly set an extra place.

~~~

The table couldn't possibly hold another bowl or plate. Vegetables, platters of turkey, saucers of mint jelly and sweet berry preserves crowded together.

"Fine feast, Aggie," Mr. Wilson said.

Mama's face beamed with pleasure. She handed Arthur a heaping plate which he carried to his small table near the stove.

Sadie remained standing, watching her family sit at their places around the table. Her legs trembled knowing that after all the trouble she caused with the fire, she was going to make more. But, she reminded herself bravely, she was doing a good deed, like a Knight of the Round Table.

"Sit down, Sadie," Mrs. Wilson said. "We're ready for the blessing."

"Mama, Dad," Sadie began. Her voice squeaked and broke, so she tried again. "Mama, Dad. I think Arthur should eat with us..." The baby gurgled loudly and banged a spoon on the wood table. Sadie raised her voice. "At the table with us from now on..."

Her words trailed off. Everyone stared at her, even Arthur. Mama's face was as bleak and frozen as pond ice. Only Grandma Wilson smiled.

"He's been here near six months now, and he shouldn't always have to eat alone."

Mr. Wilson looked down at his plate, then across the table to Sadie's mother. "He's a good worker, Aggie," he said.

"He's a Home boy, Mama," Laura complained loudly. "I don't want—"

"Be still, Laura," Mrs. Wilson said sharply.

Sadie watched them miserably. First she had ruined their house and now their Christmas. But this was important. She could feel deep inside that this mattered. A lot. Her heart thudded painfully.

"His mother was a school teacher. That's respectable. But she's dead and he doesn't have any family now and I think we should be his family. He's named after a noble and honorable king." Grandma had said to ask her. She'd tried once, but it hadn't worked. She'd have to try again. "You were an orphan, Mama. You must understand a bit how Arthur feels."

She couldn't think of anything else to say. Mama's face remained stony. Sadie felt her body sag with weariness. It had all been for nothing.

"My father went off and left my mother and me alone when I was eleven," Sadie's mother said quietly. "There one day and gone the next. He drank a great deal and I was relieved to see him gone. When I was thirteen my mother died and her sister took me in. Not out of any kind feeling on her part, just to have help with the house. My aunt never let me forget that everything I ate and everything I wore was due to her generosity. She never let me forget the shame and disgrace of being nobody's child." She looked around the table at each of them in turn, then went on. "Having Arthur here forced me to relive feelings I thought I'd long put aside. I was afraid he'd remind our neighbors of who I really was and would bring shame to all of you. But I believe now that the shame really belongs to my aunt."

The only sound in the kitchen was Lizzie slapping her hands gleefully in her mushed beans.

"My mother liked to read verses too, Sadie. Maybe you get that from her."

She suddenly nodded her head and Sadie's father cleared his throat. "Arthur," he said. "Seems Sadie's set a place for you."

∾∾∾

Sadie sighed, staring out the window at the huge flakes of snow whitening the yard. Would the waiting never end? Laura and Amy had gone to bed, too full of Christmas. Mama was upstairs settling the baby, while Arthur and Dad bedded down the animals for the night. Only Grandma remained in the kitchen, chin resting on her chest, snoring lightly. The room seemed brighter now to Sadie. The secret's shadows gone, having no reason to linger any more. Sadie knew she would take Mama's story out again and again to examine it every which way, but she had to sort something else out first.

She quietly tiptoed to the door of Arthur's room. She winced at a sudden whiff of smoke, but shrugged knowing in time it would go. The small table, taken that evening from beside the stove, was squeezed in at the end of Arthur's bed. As she stared at it, Sadie felt happiness tingle in her toes and spread warm through her body. Smiling broadly she returned to the kitchen.

"Well?" Grandma demanded.

"He's put the picture of his mother back up," Sadie said. "Seems he's decided to stay."

My name is John. I was born on April 20th, 1908 in London, England nowhere near Buckingham Palace, St. Paul's Cathedral or the Tower of London or any of those fancy places you read about. I was born in Stepney County. Some people refer to it as the slums of England. My mom died in 1919. My dad, who was in poor health, found it difficult to provide for six children. That is when the Barnardo agency placed my brother and me in the orphanage. My four sisters were put into a different orphanage and were trained to be house servants. I never saw my sisters again for forty years and one sister I have never seen since we were separated in 1919.

The first thing they did was to take away our names and give us a number—my number was thirty-seven. After several slaps across my face I soon learned to respond to my number. My trip to Canada on the H.M.S. Regina was uneventful. I spent a great deal of my seven-day ocean trip on the bow of the ship. It was fascinatingly similar to a yo-yo going up and down, except the farther I went from home, the more lonesome I was.

We landed at Montreal, June 1921. We then boarded a train bound for Belleville, Ontario. My new home was Marchmont Home in Belleville. It was a treat to behold. I was called John for the first time in years. I was one of the first boys to be selected for farm work and after a short lecture on what was expected of me, for the sum of $8.00 a month, I was on my way to my new home. I enjoyed working on the farm, especially with the cows and horses, but I was homesick and lonely and sad and I cried when nobody was looking. When I was by myself, brushing down the cows, I cried all the time in secret. They never abused me in any way, but they never paid any particular attention to me, either. I wasn't family. I never did get any of the $8.00 a month for my three and a half years' of hard work, $564.00.

John Atterbury
Surviving Home Child

Reprinted with permission — Barnardo Agency

About the Author

Home Child is not the first historically-inspired middle reader by prolific writer Barbara Haworth-Attard. Her earlier work entitled *Dark of the Moon* concerning the Underground Railroad was selected for the **Our Choice** list by the Canadian Children's Book Centre. She has also published two fantasies for young readers, *The Three Wishbells* and *TruthSinger*. Ms Haworth-Attard lives in London, Ontario.